The Sacrificial Dagger

First Printing, 2023

Imprint: Imagine Nation

Imagine Nation

Chenoa, IL 61726

AuthorJenniferLush@gmail.com

This is a work of fiction. Names, characters, businesses, places, events, locales, and incidents are either the products of the author's imagination or used in a fictitious manner. Any resemblance to actual persons, living or dead, or actual events is purely coincidental.

Chapter One

Early Bird Special

Eileen looked across the sink into the mirror. The reflection looking back at her was so much older than she actually was. It was hard to believe that just three years ago she was a beautiful, married, thirty-five year old mother of an incredible ten year old son.

The day was coming up. On July 19th, it would have been exactly three years. It seemed like a lifetime ago. A life that felt to her now like it was never really hers.

There was a pounding on the door that snapped her from her thoughts. She began what she set out to do. She grabbed some paper towels from the dispenser and wetted them in the sink with a couple pumps of soap to give herself a whore's bath in the gas station women's restroom. She could hear noises outside urging her to hurry up. One of the voices was from a little girl. There was a time when she would've felt bad about making a child wait, but that time no longer existed. The change had been sudden and gradual simultaneously. Going through it, she barely noticed. It was mostly little things like not having the desire to spend all the effort on her makeup every morning. There wasn't anyone she was doing it for or any reason for her to look her best. Then it was excused by needing to save money. Cosmetics aren't cheap. One day she looked at herself and saw the dry, cracked skin from the lack of moisturizer. She barely recognized herself. The person in the mirror was old enough to be her mom or worse, her mom's much older sister. Eileen tried to avoid mirrors now whenever she could.

She finished freshening up and fished through her tote bag for a different shirt. They all reeked. It was almost wasteful to put on deodorant. Nothing would cover up the odor of her clothes. A trip to the house was overdue, but she couldn't deal with the thought of going home right now. The day was too young to ruin it.

When she was done, she walked into a stall and pushed the handle on the toilet to flush it. She wanted to at least make it believable she was in here to use the facilities as expected. She turned the faucet at the sink on once more and washed her hands then splashed some water on her face before leaving.

Walking out of the restroom, she forced a smile at the young mom who was waiting outside. The woman took a step back. Eileen was used to that kind of reaction. It wasn't intentional, plus it wasn't like she didn't know how she looked. She'd lost quite a bit of weight when she didn't have any extra pounds to begin with. The adult small tee shirt she was wearing hung off of her the way an older sibling's hand me downs looked on a child. She was barely a skeleton with flesh. The days of dressing up and looking her best were long over. Hell, she was long past the days of using make up to simply appear less frightening.

She left her car parked along the side of the gas station and headed to the diner next door. It was a twenty-four hour joint that catered mostly to truckers, and she could largely go unnoticed there. Inside, she waited to be seated.

The young waitress spied her as soon as she arrived, but ignored her for several minutes. *'Probably hoping I'll leave,'* she sighed, realizing the best she could do with her appearance wasn't all that great. She looked around for a face she recognized, but none of the usual wait staff were in sight.

Finally, the waitress walked over. "Will anyone be joining you?" she frowned.

"No, just me."

They like to stick single people at the counter like they're some kind of leper, and they might infect the rest of the customers. It was like a quarantine zone. Not this time. The waitress led her to a corner booth far away from the nearest occupied table.

'She can smell me even a few feet away.' Eileen was long past caring about other people's opinions of her. It used to matter, but she couldn't remember when that changed either.

Shortly before the waitress reached the booth she was headed to, Eileen stopped. When the waitress noticed her, she pointed and said, "I'll take booth twelve, thanks."

Eileen sat down without giving the waitress a chance to respond. *'She's new.'* she thought as the waitress set the menu down in front of her. *'The other girls just motion for me to take a seat in my booth when they see me at the door.'*

She pulled her cell phone and charger from her tote bag and plugged it in under the table. This was her booth for a reason. She was far from homeless, but anymore she lived like she was.

The menu wasn't necessary, and she pushed it away from her. She stared out the window until the waitress returned. From where she sat, she could keep an eye on her car. This neighborhood wasn't ideal for leaving your vehicle even if it was locked.

Eileen ordered her usual coffee with ice water then added a side of whole wheat toast. When she placed her order, she put a few crumpled ones into the waitress's hand and asked to pay the bill now. The waitress did more than frown at her. She walked away from the table looking around, looking for someone. *'Probably hoping she can kick me out, or at least get a manager over here to talk to me.'* The diner had an early bird special which meant the cup of coffee was only ninety-nine cents from the hours of five to seven in the morning.

She was treating herself today. Most of the time she skipped breakfast unless there was something she could munch on in the car. Some days she had leftovers she managed to smuggle out of whatever food kitchen she had gone to the night before, or the crumbs from a bag of chips she succeeded to wrestle out of a vending machine by reaching up through the slot.

Today she would have to go home. It had been long enough, almost four weeks. Every time she left the house it took her longer to go back. Perhaps because she knew there would come a day when she wouldn't be able to go home ever again, but really it was the memories haunting her which made her want to stay away. Those memories followed her wherever she went, but the house illustrated them for her in more vivid ways.

She was almost completely out of cash. There wasn't much left at the house, but there were a few things she hadn't sold yet.

The toast tasted like the most exquisite delicacy, and her stomach churned in response to having food at an unusual hour. It was tough to say if her gut's reaction was from hunger, or if her body forgot what to do with breakfast when she ate it. She nibbled at it, trying to savor every bite.

The cries from her mid-section continued. It was both happy for the rare breakfast, and at the same time, it demanded a full meal for once. She tried to ignore its cries.

Eileen found herself staring out the window, daydreaming of a different time. It was her other life. A stranger's life that was lived in an eight bedroom estate valued at over a million dollars. There had been a team of landscapers to care for the grounds, and a maid who came three days a week.

She had a husband she loved back then. Well, a husband she loved at one time. She was sure she did way back when their relationship was new. They got married, and for a little while after that, she was certain there was love, but she couldn't remember it. All she could remember feeling for the man now was hatred and contempt. She was just as certain he had never loved her.

There was an energetic little boy who would come bouncing down the stairs full of light and life. "Mom. Mom! Today's the day!" he yelled as he entered the kitchen.

"Yes," she smiled. "It's today." He had been looking forward to this day for two months, counting down the days until little league began again.

"Come on, mom! Aren't we going?"

She laughed at him. "Sign ups aren't for another five hours."

"I know, but I want to go," he moaned dramatically.

Eileen shook her head. "We're going after lunch."

"Lunch?" he cried.

"Yes. As soon as we're finished with lunch, we'll sign you up."

His shoulders slumped. "I haven't even had breakfast yet."

"Then I guess you better get in here and eat."

There was a crash in the restaurant kitchen that jolted her back to reality and the low hum of the voices in the dining room greeted her again. She looked at the small plate in front of her. There were only a couple bites of toast left.

'Damn,' she thought. *'I had wanted to savor this, and I ate almost all of it blindly.'*

Eileen stirred some ice into her coffee to cool it off. She took another small bite of toast.

The waitress stopped by to check on her. "More coffee, please," she said, lifting the cup to her lips to gulp it down for the refill.

She put the last bite of toast in her mouth and closed her eyes. She thought about the days when breakfast consisted of omelets or eggs benedict, and bacon, fruit, milk, juice, and bacon. *'Oh god, bacon,'* she thought.

She kept her eyes closed until she heard the sound of coffee being poured into her cup. When she opened them, she saw the waitress had already picked up the small plate from her toast. Her stomach growled in protest, wanting her to press her finger onto each little crumb to lick them off, afraid of losing the smallest morsel of food. It hadn't happened for far too long, but somehow she found her dignity, not asking the waitress to leave the nearly empty plate. She smiled at the waitress to say thank you then added more ice to the mug to cool it off.

Taking a sip, she glanced around the restaurant. The place was going to start emptying soon. It was after seven now. The special was over. There were still a handful of truck drivers and an elderly couple near the front. When she glanced their way, she saw the woman's eyes quickly dart back down to her plate.

This was something else she had grown accustomed to experiencing: stolen stares. There were always looks of disgust thrown her way. Everyone had a scowl handy to give her when they understood nothing of her story. She knew they were thinking how dare this homeless woman interrupt their breakfast by having the nerve to order food at the same diner as them.

The thought made her laugh so violently she snorted which brought all eyes on her. That made it even harder not to laugh more. Surely, they now believed she was not only homeless, but crazy to boot. She wasn't homeless, but crazy was debatable. She wondered what any of them would think if they learned she would soon drive home to her 1.4 million dollar house.

After four cups of coffee and a trip to the bathroom, she left the restaurant and walked back to her car in the gas station lot. She turned on her phone. There should be enough of a charge by now to check her messages. Forty-two notifications, and almost all of them were from Remus.

Chapter Two
Just Breathe

It was typical. The longer he went without hearing from her the more often he would call. Her phone had been dead for two days. It surprised her the number wasn't higher. Another person, a more whole person, might feel thankful to have someone who worried about them. All it did for Eileen was cause her more stress.

And, there was always the nagging doubt about his true intentions. They had become friends. He was the closest she had left to a friend at least, but she often wondered why he stayed close to her. Nearly two years of searching and a small fortune spent. It had turned up empty for her, but Remus had found a number of profitable items and made new business contacts. His wallet was thick while she collected cans off the backroads to recycle for pocket change.

'It was worth it.' Her depression didn't ask for much. The bottom line was she had never been alone. Physically, yes, she was almost always by herself, but Remus was there for her whenever she needed him. He was there even when she didn't want him around.

They had talked about a timetable. Eileen had promised him, swore on everything she hoped to have in the future because swearing on everything she owned wouldn't amount to much. "If you don't hear from me for three full calendar days, I promise I will find a way to contact you first thing on day four."

It wasn't good enough for Remus. He wanted to talk to her

at least once a day, preferably twice: in the morning and again in the evening. It didn't have to be a phone call. It could be a text, email, anything to let him know she was still alive. Eileen couldn't handle it.

There were times when she forgot to eat or find a place to wash up. She'd gone a week without even taking a baby wipe to clean the stench off of her and deodorant was a luxury she couldn't always afford. There were days when breathing was all she had enough energy to accomplish. It was too much to put this on her. Forcing her to add checking in to the list of necessities for her daily routine was equal to asking her to get a job and return to a normal life. Both were equally daunting.

The anxiety in her chest swelled over returning Remus' call. It would be better to get it over with so she wouldn't have it nagging at her, lurking over her shoulder like a growing dark shadow ready to consume her.

She connected her phone to the blue tooth in her SUV. It was one of the few things she hadn't sold. It had been tempting to sell it for a junker, and she'd been able to get a fair amount of cash out of the deal as well. The only reason she kept it in the beginning was because she wasn't ready to give up all the luxuries she was used to having. Keeping it wound up benefiting her in more than one way. It was actually quite comfortable for sleeping. Even though it was four years old, the price tag on it made it easy for her to park in the more affluent neighborhoods of town to get some shut eye. No one ever questioned it. If she had attempted to ever park a twenty year old rust bucket on one of those streets, the cops would have been called without hesitation.

Once she pulled out on the road, she cycled through

Remus's voice mails.

"Hey, Eileen. It's Remus. Give me a call."

"Hey, it's me. Call me when you can."

"Hey, it's Remus. Again. Haven't heard from you in a bit. I'm worried. Call me."

"Hey! I need you to call me as soon as you get this."

"Eileen! Call me! ASAP!"

Before she got to the next message, her phone rang. It was Remus. She steered her car onto the on ramp of the interstate to make the drive north to home while she answered it. "I was going to call you. I promise. I was still making my way through your voice mails."

"I found it," he told her.

A wave of shock washed over her as the thrilling realization of his words settled into her bones. The hairs on the back of her neck stood up. Goosebumps prickled her arms, and a shiver went down her spine. This was the call she'd been hoping for every single day, and it was the call she'd come to think she'd would never receive.

"Did you hear me?" he asked when she didn't say anything.

"Yeah, I heard you." Her voice was low and hesitant. "Are you sure?'

"Yes," he said. "One hundred percent sure this is it."

She said with tears in her eyes, "Finally."

"Finally," he repeated. "And what's more? I have it."

Adrenaline pumped through her veins as she read the overhead exit signs. She was trying to figure out what would be the quickest way to get back to the west side of the city she just left. *Why didn't I just call him before I started to drive?*

Nothing had ever felt this urgent. She had to get to the

shop, to Remus, and she needed to be there now. It was finally happening. Her entire body shook, and the interstate blurred from the wetness in her eyes. A screaming horn barreling passed shocked her awake to realize she'd been easing her foot off the gas. She needed to focus on getting there, and in her excited and terrified state, it was going to take her full attention to do it.

Remus started to tell her there was no need to rush. He was still translating the hieroglyphics. It would take time until he was ready because he could only work on it in between customers. He was talking long after Eileen had stopped listening.

She had already pressed the button to end the call. It wouldn't matter if he had told her he still had to chisel it out of a thousand pounds of concrete. There was no way he could tell her he had it, the item she spent the better part of two years traveling the globe trying to find, and not expect her to head to his shop immediately.

Two missed turns and thirty-five minutes later, she parked her car just around the corner from Remus's shop. It felt like an eternity had passed since their phone call. The urgency racing through her was hard to quell. If she ran into the shop like this, breathing hard, shaking, and barely able to form a coherent sentence, he wouldn't let her have it.

Her hands white knuckled the steering wheel and probably had been since she ended the call. She pried them off, opening and closing her fingers to relax them and work out the built up tension in her joints. Her fingernails were short from serving as tools and caked with dirt underneath. She needed a real shower. She focused on her breaths, in through the nose and out through the mouth. *'There was a process,'* she reminded herself. Nothing was going to happen right now in that shop. It wasn't quite dark enough yet for her liking either.

"But it's finally here." Her voice squeaked, barely audible. Her body rocked back and forth, and she felt the sob rising in her throat, blocking her ability to breathe for a moment, before breaking free in a heart wrenching moan.

'No,' she told herself. *'There's no time for a breakdown.'*

That could come later. Once she had it in her possession and was in the privacy of her home, she could lose it for as long as she needed. Until then, she had to collect herself.

Shallow breaths like she used in labor helped erase the tears. She shook out her arms and cracked her neck on side then turning to repeat it on the other. She talked to herself. Nothing important. She read the warning label on her visor about air bags and young children sitting in the front seat.

That one almost got her. Noah had never been old enough to sit up front, and he had been counting down the days until he could, "ride like a grown up."

There was an old receipt floating around between the front seats. She picked it up reading the details of the $3.27 she had put in her gas tank waiting for her voice to return to normal.

She watched the street light on the corner flicker and wondered if it was some sort of omen. She knew what she was going to have to do, but there had always been a seed of doubt in her mind if she'd be able to go through with it. She had a long time to prepare for this, but part of her had always treated it like a dark fairy tale. It was a distant morbid fantasy, not something which would ever come to fruition. Her hands were shaking, and she felt like she might get sick. Her nervousness was making it difficult to do anything except breathe.

Eileen got out of the car after several minutes of psyching herself up to do it and walked down the street toward the shop. She passed the displays of incense, candles and kitchen witch type of books in the window. If you didn't know better, you might think the Mystic Treasures shop only catered to bored housewives and teenagers who had read one too many fluff books about the supernatural.

Those customers could get under Remus's skin easily enough. He would roll his eyes when he talked about them. His words dripping with disdain. He had to humor them because they paid the bills. They would come in and easily drop a couple hundred or more on everything they needed to set up their own spell casting at home.

Remus was well aware they'd toy around with their purchase for a couple weeks until they realized life wasn't that simple even with the help of amateur magic. It would take a lot more than a spell to lose twenty pounds before their anniversary next month. An imaginary love potion number nine wouldn't do anything to cause the cute boy in history class to fall in love with someone. Their purchase would be shoved aside in a box somewhere collecting dust until it was finally thrown out or sold at a garage sale.

He would feel bad about taking their money if it wasn't what kept his lights turned on. The serious inquiries, the ones that made him the real cash, were random and weren't reliable enough to guarantee he stayed in business. If you were one of the few who did know what the store really had to offer, you could accomplish anything your heart desired by asking the right questions.

She pushed the door open, and stepped inside. The bell hanging overhead to alert Remus of a new customer.

Chapter Three
The Recording

Naomi arranged the items on the little table for the third time since Eileen sat down. She tried not to judge the self-professed medium. The woman had come highly recommended. It could be obsessive compulsion causing her to constantly mess with the tools of the trade before beginning, or it could be her just being thorough, making sure nothing was forgotten.

Whatever it was, Eileen was growing impatient. The charge was for an hour, and the minutes were already ticking away. This woman better be planning an hour from when she begins the actual reading, not an hour for the appointment time which Eileen had been generously early when arriving.

Various contacts she had made during her search for answers, more like reassurances, had highly recommended Naomi. It took over a month to get in for this session. Weeks of excruciating agony for Eileen as she tried not to be too hopeful this woman was it. She didn't want to get crushed again like the long list of others she'd gone to before her.

The weeks had been made with promises to herself that this would be the last one. If Naomi turned out to be a con artist too, she'd never go to another psychic. They were empty threats. She'd made them before and never followed through.

'Just start!' She screamed the words inside her while plastering a fake, friendly smile on her face.

Naomi left the room. "I'll be right back," she said. The

strings of beads in the otherwise open doorway shook their way back into place.

Eileen rubbed her temples trying to pull the tension out of her mind. *'If this woman doesn't hurry up already,'* she stopped herself from finishing the menacing vow. Instead she said a small form of prayer. Not to God. Oh, no. God had turned his back on her over a year ago. She spoke quietly to her son in her mind. *'Please, Noah. Please be here today. Let me know you're okay.'*

"Would you like a recording?"

She opened her eyes, surprised to see the woman. The beads hadn't announced her return to the small room on the side of the house decked out in new age décor.

The woman sat a small tape recorder on the table. Eileen nodded and waited for the woman to give her a price. It'd probably be another five dollars for the recording in addition to the twenty dollars minimum she'd have to drop to buy a device and batteries if she ever wanted to listen to it.

'Ten dollars?' It was impossible to hide her frustration when Naomi told her the cost. Her eyes rolled hard enough to make her dizzy. None of the other psychics had ever charged more than five for a recording, not that all of them offered one. Two even threw it in as a complimentary feature which was why their standard rates were higher than the rest.

"It's good to have one to reference later. You might think you'll remember every word of every message that comes through, but you'd be surprised." She pressed record and placed it on the table. "Plus sometimes other things come through you can't hear during the reading."

"Like what?" Eileen asked.

The woman raised her shoulders. "Oh anything. Could be voices. That's happened before. Or other strange sounds like something being moved or knocking."

Eileen wasn't sure what any of it meant. She didn't want to spend the time thinking about it either. All she wanted was to find out if this woman could contact Noah. The recording was in progress which meant they were finally starting. *'Took her long enough.'* She glanced at her watch. Nine minutes had already passed.

"When you listen to the playback, just pay attention to when the other noises come through if there are any. That's usually when the spirits are trying to speak."

'If you say so,' Eileen nodded. *'If only you would speak to my son instead of me.'*

"These are my crystals." The woman began after finally sitting down across from Eileen.

"They are all charged with energy which I can use to open the channels to the beyond."

'Why do they always sound so hokey?' Eileen wondered. Some people had the gift. It was something she fully believed in long before the accident. Most of them don't, and it was hard to weed through the swindlers preying on the broken hearts, isolation, and depression of their customers. She'd love to just once come to a reading and be met by someone in jeans, a t-shirt and a messy bun who simply sat and talked to her without any of the hippy-dippy nonsense thrown in for atmosphere. *'Lady, please! I want to hear from Noah!'*

"I'll be using them throughout the reading." The woman carefully took each one out of the bowl and laid them in a straight line off to one side. Their colors and shapes varied, but they were mostly close to the same size.

Eileen found herself wondering what the difference was and if it was easy to learn to use them. She could save a lot of time, money, and energy if she could do this herself at home.

Naomi laid both arms across the table with her palms up. In one hand, she held a yellowish crystal which she rolled around in her fingers. When she straightened up, she continued to play with the small stone, sometimes switching it to a different hand.

"Many are trying to come through at once," Naomi said. "They're worried about you."

'*Generic,*' Eileen thought.

"There was a separation," Naomi continued.

"Yes." Eileen acknowledge out of habit. One of these days, she'd sit through an entire session without so much as nodding her head in encouragement, but she found it was difficult not to do it.

The woman looked to the side, behind Eileen, like someone was standing there talking to her. It was another trick she had witnessed far too many times. "Yes," she went on. "You've been lonely."

Eileen exhaled deeply. She'd been waiting this whole time for nothing.

"There was a death too."

Her eyes shot up. This was why she was here. It didn't take a psychic to see the lack of rings on her fingers to assume she was single. It was her son she wanted to reach.

"The death was recent."

Eileen's eyes moistened, and she blinked rapidly to prevent the tears.

"Someone close to you. Your husband?"

She was careful not to respond. The woman was fishing to see if she could figure out who might have passed away from Eileen's responses. She'd sat through too many of these sessions to be fooled like that again.

"No," the woman said. "But connected to him."

Eileen watched her carefully, reading the psychic as well. *'Please let her be the real deal,'* she silently begged.

"Ah, yes, a child," the woman nodded.

One tear drop rolled down Eileen's cheek, and she wiped it away quickly.

"Your son."

'Maybe she knows what she's doing. She's figuring it out.' Each hopeful thought was pushed down by the skeptic living in her brain. *'It was a fifty-fifty chance. Don't buy into her yet.'*

"You're still hurting," Naomi said compassionately. "He's with you."

Naomi fiddled with the crystal and put it back on the table. She picked up a different one. "I need something stronger to help him come through clearly."

By the end of the session, Eileen was convinced. Noah had come through. She felt the calmest she had since the accident. Her son was in a good place.

Days later, Eileen walked out of the discount super store unable to wait until she reached her SUV to tear into the plastic wrapping around the voice recorder. One of her nails broke and her finger smarted from the cut. *'Why do they make these things so difficult to open?'*

She rummaged through her SUV hoping to find something sharp enough to get through the indestructible packaging. There was a small travel tool kit in the glove compartment. It was one of Johnny's notoriously thoughtless gifts. He had laughed at her reaction. *'Oh, haha,'* she thought at the time. *'Waste my money on something which will never be used.'*

"I guess I was wrong, Johnny." She muttered to herself as she stabbed through the plastic with a screwdriver. "Your gift finally came in handy."

Eileen ripped the voice recorder free and opened the batteries, spilling half of them on the floorboard. She'd get them later. The mini-cassette had been floating around her purse since she left the session with Naomi, and she found it.

It only took days of looking to find one. They weren't heavily stocked anymore, not like they were in the nineties when everyone was using them. People recorded notes on their phones now.

The reading had gone much better than she ever imagined. There were only a few times when she gave away information or let Naomi know what she said was accurate. This medium said things she couldn't possibly have known. It had to be the real deal.

It began to play while Eileen drove home. There was some scuffling at first, but Naomi had stretched on the table. That was probably what she was hearing. Then she heard the knocking. It came shortly after Naomi figured out the recent loss was a child.

'It's Noah!' The revelation made her happy, not sad. She beamed, knowing he came through. It was really him. He was still with her. It was the most comfort she'd had, the only comfort she'd had since losing him.

Half of the session had played before she began to figure it out. The knocks were louder when she was upset or when the messages delivered were heavy. They were softer at other parts.

'*It was the crystals,*' she realized. '*That fake played with the crystals in her hands and gently hit them on the table.*' The sound had been too soft for Eileen to notice, especially when concentrating on what Naomi was saying at the time. Hitting the table within inches of the recorder made the sounds come through on the cassette loud and clear.

Eileen hit her hand on the wheel until it hurt, and she screamed loudly. The people passing on the road couldn't hear her, nor would she have cared if they did. Her tears busted through the damn, and she couldn't control them. Her heart physically hurt from the pain of being taken again.

'*How can these people live with themselves? Taking advantage of people already in a weakened state like this?*'

Her voice flowed into her ears. The tape was at the part where she told Naomi it brought her great joy to hear Noah was at peace. The tone of her voice was high pitched and filled with emotion.

"She took advantage of me!" she screamed.

Eileen rolled her window down and threw the voice recorder out into the road. It held up pretty good which intensified her anger. The car behind her clipped the corner of it, busting it apart and sent it into the opposite lane of traffic. It was hit again by the car that just passed her, leaving a black and silver busted mess in the middle of the road with the brown tape flying in the breeze.

Chapter Four

Hidden Artifact

"I'll be right with you," Remus said before turning to see it was Eileen. He gave her a quick wave then finished ringing up the items for the woman at the counter.

Eileen walked over and browsed the incense as though she were a regular customer. She could hear Remus's sing-song customer service voice carry throughout the store as he handed out a few last pieces of advice to the woman. He was polite and friendly to their faces. They'd never guess how heartily he made fun of them later when they were gone.

There were four slots for dragon's blood, and she scrunched up her nose. It smelled disgusting in her opinion, and she never understood the attraction to it. The overwhelming scent of all the varieties assaulted her nostrils, and she stifled a couple sneezes.

The woman finished her transaction and headed to the door. Eileen saw two bags packed tight as she walked passed. When the door closed behind the woman, Eileen turned and shot Remus a look.

He shrugged, "Hey. I got to eat too."

She walked to the counter and asked, "Where is it?"

"It's in the back. I'll grab it," he told her. "I tried telling you before you so rudely hung up on me," he said, walking toward the back of the store. "There was no rush. I'm not done translating it yet."

He disappeared into the back for only a minute before

returning through the doorway. "You're going to love this though," he said, carrying a small box. "There was a reason we had so much trouble locating it."

Remus placed the small wooden box on the counter and lifted the lid. He removed a large, rather gaudy looking bracelet from it. It was at least six inches long and would cover most of the lower arm of anyone who wore it. There were markings on the sides that looked like hieroglyphs. In the center of it was a large Egyptian eye. It was mostly a solid sheath except for small intricate cut outs adding to the design.

"During the Crusades, they hid the dagger in the best possible place," he said, setting the overly ornate bracelet on the counter. "They hid it in a bracelet." Remus pushed on the center of the eye, and a dagger shot out from the end of it.

Eileen jumped and laughed nervously, holding her hand to her chest. It was brilliant! Remus was probably right too. This was why they couldn't find the dagger. They were looking for the wrong thing all along. Eileen picked it up and looked it over. It was as amazing as it was ugly.

He pushed the eye again while she held it, and the dagger retracted. "Here," he said, taking it from her. He clasped the bracelet around one arm and dropped his wrist, holding his hand downward away from the edge of the metal. He pressed the eye with his other hand, and the dagger shot out again. "Ingenious, isn't it?"

All this time they had been searching for a dagger, a weapon. It was no wonder so many doors were shut in their face by people telling them the sacrificial dagger had been destroyed almost a thousand years ago by the Christians during the Crusades. There was document after document claiming it had been successfully hidden, but no one believed it to be true. No one except Remus, and he managed to convince Eileen not to give up. It was because of him she kept searching, spending a small fortune on tracking it down long after her hope of finding it faded.

When he removed it from the box, she reached for it again and slid it on her arm with far less effort than it took Remus. The bracelet might have been made to be adjustable. The two long sides could probably bend for a tighter fit, or be pulled out depending on the size of the person's arm. As old as it was, Eileen didn't dare take the chance of the metal snapping if she tried to adjust it.

It hung loosely and slid around her arm as she moved. That wouldn't matter. She didn't plan on wearing it for show. She only needed to use the dagger, and it didn't have to be on her arm when she did.

"Let me," he said, reaching for it again.

"What does it say?" she asked, handing it to him.

"I'm a little rusty on my Ancient Egyptian. It's going to take time. I've made photo copies to enlist some help. There are a couple people I know who could translate it faster than me, but they'll expect payment."

"You know I don't care about the cost."

Remus reminded her, "You will when the well runs dry."

It was true. Her fortune was almost gone. In recent months, doubts started to creep in about what would happen if she hadn't found a solution before she was too broke to continue the search. She pushed the thoughts from her mind as soon as they entered. Doubt led to failure, and that wasn't an option.

He held the bracelet in front of her and pointed to one of the images. "The corner of this one has broken off." He rolled it to the other side of the eye and showed her another one that had experienced so much wear the image was rubbed down and couldn't easily be made out.

The bell above the shop door rang. Another customer had entered. Remus set the bracelet back in the box and greeted the man who had entered the store.

He was older, probably in his mid-fifties. Remus started to come out from the counter asking, "May I help you find anything?"

The man made a beeline straight to him. "A buddy of mine told me to come here," he said, approaching Remus. He was almost to the counter before he took notice of Eileen, and he hesitated.

Remus followed his gaze to her. "It's alright. She's a colleague."

He shifted his weight uncomfortably, and said, "I'm looking... I'm looking for..." He glanced back toward Eileen then stood straight, building his courage and told Remus, "I'm looking for wolf's blood."

"Ah," Remus said with a slow nod. "For impotency."

The man's eyes widened, and he reeled backward.

"I am so sorry, sir," Remus told him, looking at Eileen frantically. "I assure you the privacy of my customers is very important to me. I'm just so comfortable talking freely around Eileen," he explained, glancing at her again.

The customer turned to her. Humiliation blanketed his face.

"My husband has used it." She forced a weak smile at him.

"It does the trick," she lied. Maybe one area of their marriage would've been enjoyable if she had learned about wolf's blood when they were together.

He seemed satisfied and looked back at Remus. "So you have some?" he asked.

"I do. It's in the fridge in the back. I'll only be a minute."

Remus went into his stock room in the back and returned with a small Styrofoam container. "How much do you need?"

"I'm not sure. The instructions don't specify an amount."

"Sprinkle it, right?" Remus asked.

"Yes, but it doesn't tell you if that's a few drops or a couple tablespoons." The man gave Eileen another nervous glance. It couldn't be easy discussing his problems with erectile dysfunction in front of a woman.

Remus nodded, understanding his frustration. This was not the first customer in his store with this exact question. "That's because it will vary on each person's needs. Unfortunately, I can't give you an amount either. Take into consideration your own personal struggles and what your desired outcome will be. Make a best guess in that exact range: a few drops to a couple tablespoons."

"You want to error on the side of caution, however. If you go to the hospital with a complication from Viagra, the staff will be understanding and know what to do. It's much more difficult to walk into a hospital with complications from wolf's blood. The best I can advise you is to be cautious, and if it doesn't work, try again in a month using a little more blood."

He pulled out two bags of blood from inside. They were the standard blood bags used in hospitals everywhere.

"How do you even get wolf's blood?" the man asked. "You

know what? I don't want to know."

"How much do you think you'll need?" Remus asked. "I sell it by the pint and half pint. I don't offer a discount for the larger size. Two half pint bags would cost the same as one full bag. If you want to start with the smaller amount and come back later if you need more, I always have it in stock."

"No," the man said. "It was an eight hour drive to get here. I hope I don't have to come back. No offense."

Remus smiled at him. That was hardly anything to be upset about. His shop stood out from others like it in that he actually had the rare and exotic, the magical ingredients, the outrageous and the common too. His was the only shop on this side of the country where most of the special stock was located off the floor and had to be asked for specifically was sold. Half the phone calls and emails he received every day was asking if he offered shipping. It'd double his profit, but the investigations opened for him if any of the packages were checked weren't worth it.

He rang up the purchase and packaged the blood with cold packs, giving the man explicit instructions on how to keep it fresh. After the man left, Remus closed the container. "I've got to get this back in the refrigerator," he said, leaving Eileen alone in the store.

He made his way to the back and put the cooler on the shelf in the fridge when he heard the shop bell ring again. It had been busy today. "I'll be right with you," he hollered loudly from the back room.

When he emerged from the doorway, he looked around the store, but he didn't see anyone, and that included Eileen. He ran to the counter and looked in the box. The bracelet was gone.

He went out the front door of the shop and checked the sidewalks in both directions, but he didn't spy her. Tires squealed near the intersection on the corner. He turned just in time to see Eileen's SUV speed away.

Remus instinctively reached for his phone as he walked back inside, but thought better of it. She wouldn't answer. Not now. He couldn't exactly call the police. If they located the dagger, it would wind up in a museum not back in his hands. The dagger was stolen. By who and from where Remus didn't have a clue. For something that old and that valuable to be on the market, it had to be gained through elicit means.

Eileen had been through so much. She had spent millions of dollars searching through centuries of the occult desperately seeking something to help her with her son. To say she wanted the dagger would be an understatement. She needed it like she needed oxygen to breathe.

The empty box stared back at him from the counter, and he shook his head. He should've known.

Chapter Five
Rundown Estate

Eileen parked at the end of the long drive that led to her home. She got out and walked up to the gate, tugging on it with all the strength she could muster and scraped it open until there was enough room to drive through. She debated about closing it behind her or leaving it as it was. Her energy was zapped, but she knew if she didn't, she would regret it. This would be the day someone would come by to deliver a notice, a summons over some long overdue bill. It took her three times as long to shut it, and she was out of breath by the time she was back behind the wheel.

She pulled around the circle drive in front of her home and looked at the weeds and vines that were overgrown. The estate property hadn't been mowed and cared for properly in well over two years. The first twelve years she lived there it never stopped aweing her every time she made it past the trees along the lane that gave way to the beautiful two story brick home.

Now it only reminded her of death. Even if the grounds were still being looked after, it wouldn't change her opinion. No matter how elegant the home might look on the outside, it wouldn't erase the ghosts that lurked behind the door. It was better this way, having it look forlorn and filled with despair. There wouldn't be any surprises when the day came for someone to force their way inside looking for her, expecting to find a body rotting on the floor.

The phone laying on the passenger seat seamed to scream

at her as if it had a voice of its own. It was intentionally placed face down, so she wouldn't see the attempts Remus made at getting ahold of her. She felt bad for stealing the bracelet, but wondered if it was really theft. It was her money that backed the search. Several million dollars had been shelled out to find something that would work, and a large percent of that money had been funneled through Remus.

It took over a half hour for her to build the courage to go inside. She tried to convince herself to do it by saying she wouldn't need this home much longer, and she would only be here for a short period of time. Each time she pumped herself up, the evil voice inside her head would point out it would be at least an overnight visit. She'd have to start over again.

Finally, she drug herself from the car and grabbed her oversized tote and book bag from the backseat. She headed up the steps to the front door and unlocked all four padlocks she installed on the outside of the door. Not that it mattered. The alarm system was disabled. All anyone would have to do was break a window, and they'd be home free.

She hadn't stepped completely inside before she heard her son's laughter down the hall and winced from the pain. The days of happiness ended years ago, but this home always haunted her with the memories. She'd give anything, was giving everything, to hear his contagious laughter again.

In the front room, she cleaned out the fireplace to start a fire. It was far too hot outside to need one, but without utilities, it was the only way to get things done. Her stockpile of firewood was getting low, but for once, she wasn't worried about it. This would hopefully be the last time she was back here.

Once the fire was lit, she walked to the back of the house. The soles of her tennis shoes weren't enough to prevent the echoing of her footsteps in the empty mansion. Every spirit who crouched in wait and every rodent who sought refuge in these walls were being warned of an intruder.

Off the back porch, she removed the tarp from the wagon that had her three largest pots from the kitchen nestled inside of it. She pulled it fifty yards to the old pump on the property. Johnny had wanted to have it removed. He thought it was an eyesore. Eileen thought it was quaint. It was one of the things she liked about the property. It was a good thing for her now that she won the argument, and the pump had stayed.

She cranked the handle and rinsed the webs and dead bugs out of the pots. They could only be filled a little over halfway. Anything more and the water would just slosh over the tops as she pulled the wagon around the front of the house. She carried them one by one inside before taking them down the hall to the bathroom.

It was tiny, but at least it had a tub. It was much easier than carrying the pots upstairs. She took an old towel and wiped the cobwebs out then put the plug in the drain. The water in the pans barely covered the bottom of the tub, but it was something she had learned to work around. It was tiresome making multiple trips to the well.

She grabbed her bags and took them to the bathroom. The stench of both bags hit her when she opened them. She packed her clean clothes in the tote, and when they became too ripe, she put them in the book bag. The clothes always wound up mixed together no matter what she did to be careful. She dumped both bags on the floor, separating the clothes from her other necessities.

The detergent was still in the car. All she wanted to do was sleep, and she considered washing them with bar body soap, but decided it would take too long. She went out and opened the back hatch of her SUV. There was an assortment of empty detergent containers she had rummaged from various trash cans. She grabbed one and brought it inside.

She took the cap off and lowered it into the tub, filling it with as much water as she could. With the cap back on, she shook it vigorously, getting all the remnants of soap that clung to the sides. She poured it into the tub, and swished the water around with her hands. It looked like it would be enough, so she added her clothes to let them soak.

Then she went back to the well to fill them a second time. There would be at least four trips out here tonight because she desperately needed a bath. This time she set the pans just inside the front door to get the fire ready for them.

Eileen took the rack from her oven that was leaning against the side of the fireplace and positioned it inside over the flames. She had been pleased to learn it was an almost perfect fit the first night she tried it after the gas was shut off.

After putting all three pots on the rack to boil, she went into the kitchen and rummaged through the cabinets. There wasn't much there, and most of it she wasn't hungry enough to attempt to eat. She found a can of ravioli and turned it around. It was two months expired, but she had eaten worse. The manual can opener was still on the counter from her last visit, and she cut off the lid. She leaned against the counter with a fork, eating it cold out of the can.

Dust danced in the beams of the light that shown through

the large patio doors off of where the dining room had once been. The room was now bare. The ornate dining set consisting of a table, chairs, hutch and buffet she used to own was one of the first things she sold. Without a family, there was no need for a family table.

When she looked in the vacant room, she could still see it. The table was meticulously set. Thanksgiving dinner proudly laid out with a beautifully roasted turkey near Johnny's seat for him to carve. She could even see herself walking around the table, making last minute adjustments to the display. Her son was antsy, and she told him to sit over and over again. Even if he listened to her, he'd be up in a few seconds, running to the door to see if his dad was home yet because he couldn't wait to eat.

Johnny had to run to the office to grab a few things even though it was Thanksgiving. She knew. Deep down she had always known, but she had accepted the lies. It worked for them. Both of them got what they wanted. They were the perfect devoted parents and spouses in public. Behind closed doors, he had the lifestyle he wanted which included a mistress, and she had her son. He was the whole world to her.

It was when she stopped accepting the lies that everything fell apart. It was the day she had enough. It was the day she decided to call Johnny out on what he was doing. She was tired of being used by him for her money and her prominent standing in the city and decided to do something about it. That was the day her world ended.

That wasn't the whole truth. Noah was growing up. He didn't need her like he had when he was a baby. They were still very close, but every day, she saw a little more independence in him. It wouldn't be long until he went to college, was off on his own, falling in love, and beginning a life for himself away from this home. It was still years away, but Eileen could feel it coming.

It was thinking about her own future which made her act. She would have nothing when Noah left. There was no way to move on, to fill the void his absence would leave, while she was still married to Johnny. That's what motivated her. There had to be a better life waiting for her out there somewhere.

She set the empty can on the counter and walked back to the door to grab the bracelet from her tote. She pressed the eye again, revealing the dagger. It looked dull which was a disappointment, but not a surprise. She held the bracelet and lightly jabbed at her leg. It indented her skin and there was a small pain from the pressure, but it wasn't sharp enough to break the skin.

Her kitchen was mostly bare, and she didn't think she'd find what she needed. Still she searched. Every cabinet, every drawer was given a once over until she found it. It wasn't the style she used in her past life, so it was almost overlooked. It was a long metal wedge with a gripped handle more resembling a comical pirate's sword than a knife sharpener. She painstakingly used it to work the edges of the blade until the dagger cut everything she tested. From her hair, to paper, to the counter, to her own skin, the dagger cut through everything easily.

The downstairs was heating up, and she was sweating from the fire in the next room. She checked on the pans. The water was just starting to bubble. She carried them to the bathroom and dumped them in the tub. The bathroom sink held a small array of kitchen utensils, and she grabbed the two pairs of wide ended plastic salad tongs to use to agitate the clothes before leaving them to soak longer. The pans had to be brought back to the pump to fetch water for rinsing.

After her clothes were clean, she wrung them out and bundled them in her arms to carry them to the back porch where she had a makeshift clothesline. She had found a brand new package of bungee cords in the garage which she strung together between opposite corner beams for her laundry. She wrung out each piece one more time over the rail and draped them over the line. It would be a miracle if they were dry by morning.

The water for her bath was already on the fire. She dumped the boiling water into the tub then collected cold water from the well. She added it in slowly to bring down the temperature. The remaining water she poured into the toilet tank, so she could flush it later when she needed.

When she slid into the bath, it no longer had the relaxing feel that it used to give her. It wasn't because of the extra work that went into it, but because she knew she didn't deserve to relax. Not after what she had done. Not until she pieced the shattered fragments of her world back together. It felt like she was doing something wrong whenever she took five minutes to herself.

She dried off and took the old robe from the door to wrap around her. Neither the towel nor the robe had been washed in close to two years, and she couldn't help but laugh. Even the people who believed in hanging a towel to dry so it could be reused would think her gross.

Eileen walked up the stairs and went to the guest bedroom.

There were a few boxes of odds and ends stored along the wall. It was all the possessions she had left in the world. Most of it wasn't worth anything which is why they weren't already sold. There were a few paintings leaning next to them she had held onto, hoping to keep them. It was time to let them go. She needed the money, and she wouldn't be able to take them on the plane.

Farther down the hallway, she lingered outside Noah's room. She put her hand on the doorknob, but couldn't bear to go inside. His room wasn't touched. It was exactly the way he left it. She couldn't bring herself to get rid of anything that had been his. She couldn't bring herself to go into the room at all. Even though she knew she would see him again soon, she couldn't face it. She couldn't face his memory head on until she had to, until she could actually face him.

She walked to the end of the hall where the master bedroom was and went into the closet. The back panel could be removed to reveal a small room. It once housed Johnny's safe, but he took it with him when they separated. The only thing there now was a duffel bag. She had packed it and repacked it many times, praying there would be a need for it. Her prayers had finally been answered.

Taking the bag from the closet, she stopped and grabbed the paintings from the guest room. She carried them downstairs and set them by the front door. Looking at the duffel bag was liberating and made her eyes water with tears at how close she was. She didn't need to double check the contents. It would all be there.

It contained three outfits she hadn't worn since her son died and his clothes that had been in the laundry the night of the accident. The money that would let them flee the country was on the bottom, and the passports with their new identities lay on top.

Chapter Six
Pancakes

Eileen knew he was different when she walked through the door. The room he worked out of was plain, simple. There were no bells and whistles because he didn't need any. He was the real deal who didn't need a bunch of mind detracting decorations to make someone believe he was capable of accomplishing what he was selling. As she drove to the address he gave her, she went over everything just to be sure, still looking for the spot where he duped her.

Morvan loomed over her when he introduced himself, but he was no more intimidating than the wisp of a woman she was becoming. "You're alone," he said. The words were stated like fact. It wasn't a question, and the statement didn't bear with it any trace of judgement or pity.

"Very much so," she admitted.

She had looked better. Her clothes were worn. Nothing in her wardrobe had been updated in close to a year. Many people lived like this only buying necessities as the need for them arose either because they couldn't afford it or because they didn't care as much about appearances.

Anyone associated with Eileen before the accident was worried about her because she stopped caring. There were changes such as she wasn't shopping like it was a sport anymore. Her skin was usually natural instead of the hour long morning routine she previously followed meticulously to keep herself looking young and attractive. Even moisturizer had unfortunately been left behind. They saw all of this as signs she was still struggling. They saw it, they pointed it out, but no one tried to intervene or help her.

'If I saw someone looking like this, I would think they were alone too. They don't have anyone to impress, and they gave up on looking good for themselves too.'

They sat at a small wooden table. Her mind wondered what the use of it in its former life had been. It was far too large to be an accent table, but much too small for the kitchen. The size was perfect for this type of work, but she hadn't seen tables for psychic readings advertised at any furniture store she had ever visited.

There were three small pillar candles in a line across the table between them. The one in the middle was light purple, and she guessed it would fill the room with lilac or lavender when he lit it. The other two were an identical medium shade of blue. Morvan pulled a lighter from the pocket on the front of his shirt and lit the candle in the middle. A pleasing aroma wafted from it, lilacs. He placed the lighter on the table, ignoring the other two candles.

He closed his eyes and lowered his face slightly, rubbing his hands together. When he looked at her again, the reading began. That's all he did during the reading. He closed his eyes and rubbed his hands. It was fairly predictable with generalized comments almost anyone could fit to their own life until he brought up Noah.

"You lost your son?" he asked.

It wouldn't have been hard to deduce. She had already admitted to being alone. There was no wedding band on her finger. It had left a line of pale white skin when she first stopped wearing it, but that small area had since received enough sun to match the tan of the rest of her fingers.

The easy guess was either her child or her spouse had passed away. The lack of evidence showing a recent spouse gave Morvan a fifty-fifty chance choosing between son and daughter. She felt her head nod slightly in betrayal to her. *'Stop feeding him the answers,'* she pleaded.

The rest of the initial part of the reading was fairly standard too. She had lost her way, was struggling to find purpose, and felt guilty. These were all things she had heard numerous times before mostly from the therapists everyone insisted she see. For a while, she went twice a week without missing a session until she realized there was no counselor who could help her. The only thing that would help was knowing her son was okay. It had to be more than faith, more than trusting what she or someone else believed. She needed proof, and the only way she was going to get that proof was finding someone who could reach Noah.

Morvan picked up the lighter, and said, "I'm going to reach out now. There's no guarantee of who will come through, but is there anyone specific you're hoping to contact."

"My son," Eileen replied. No one else would do.

"And what is his name?"

All of the snarky comments about how he was supposed to be the psychic brewed under the surface, but she bit her tongue. "Noah," she replied softly, deciding to be content Morvan had used present tense. He still very much was her son in every way.

He lit the other two candles which smelled surprisingly of Cedarwood. He laid his arms out across the table on either side of the candles, palms turned slightly to the side, facing each other.

Eileen studied them for a moment wondering if he meant for her to take his hands. She slowly moved her hands toward his.

Morvan smiled and said, "You don't have to if you're not comfortable with it."

She put both her hands into his and concentrated on the candle flames.

"Once I make contact, you're welcome to comment. I'll probably tune most of it out." Morvan paused and chuckled. "I say that now, but I might remark to everything you say also. It depends. Just try to refrain from asking questions. It distracts me. I need intense concentration to keep the communication lines open to the other side, and something as simple as paying attention to a question could break my focus."

Eileen nodded. *'No questions. Perfect.'* It reduced the odds of leading what he told her which meant there was less chance of being conned.

"I'm going to perform something I call a vocal cleansing. I've discovered it helps clear my mind of all thoughts and create a pathway of communication. It might sound weird, but it works for me," he said with a gentle shrug.

Eileen nodded having absolutely no idea what he was talking about, but that would soon change. He began by trilling his r's in a rising crescendo. She was waiting for one good, "Arriba!" followed by a mariachi band walking through the doorway. Morvan's voice went into a low moan almost as if he was imitating how ghosts are typically portrayed in movies. That was followed by several ear shattering barks. Eileen was two seconds from snatching her hands back and leaving. He had done nothing remarkable yet, and this ridiculous display was making her feel foolish for wasting her money.

"He's here!" Morvan announced.

She paused and waited to hear more. It was taking what felt like an eternity although it was merely seconds. She fidgeted in her seat, trying to move closer, excited.

"Your son says he loves you."

Eileen's heart dropped. "I love you too, baby, I miss you." Her voice cracked as she spoke.

"He's always with you. He wants you to know that. When you're talking to him, he can hear you."

Her tears began to silently roll down her cheeks. Most of the time she could sense him. People said it all the time. "Your loved ones can hear you. You can feel them when they're close." She had never put much stock into the words until she lost Noah. When he was near, his presence was felt. He'd be all around her in one room, but gone when she moved to another. It was hard to describe, but she was certain it was him. Most of the time she believed he was trying to comfort her, to take away her pain.

"Your son wants you to know he's sorry. He shouldn't have ridden his bike home that night."

"Baby, no," Eileen said between sobs. "It's my fault. I should've answered the phone."

"He wants you to stop blaming yourself. He doesn't think it's your fault. He doesn't hold you responsible."

Eileen couldn't let go of the guilt she felt. Numerous therapists had tried. It was something she'd take to her grave. Her son needed her, and she failed him.

"He knows you go into his room to cry."

Those words sent a pain straight to her heart. His room was the one area she hadn't disturbed except when she gave in to her grief while lying on his bed. She'd imagine him playing, tearing through his toy box, making a mess again right after it'd been cleaned. It was becoming harder to picture him which added to her darkness.

It was about to overtake her. The sadness she tried to push back except for when she was alone then it hit her. Everything he'd told her was what all grieving parents want to hear. It's what people do in their grief. The only detail specific to her son was the bike accident, but it had been a high profile case captivating the local news headlines for months. Morvan had to recognize the name if not her face from all the footage of interviews.

Morvan chuckled, and said, "He's telling me about the pancakes."

Eileen squinted her eyes and straightened in her seat. *'Pancakes? We had pancakes together so often.'*

"He made you pancakes one morning. Breakfast in bed."

'Oh! How could I have forgotten?' She covered her mouth with her hand. Her heart rate increased. *'Say it, Noah. Please. Let me know it's really you.'*

"He's really laughing about this as he's telling me, so I'm getting the story in fragments."

Eileen sat at the edge of her seat waiting for more.

"He mixed up some ingredients?"

It sounded like Morvan was asking instead of telling her what Noah said. She wouldn't be tricked this time. She wasn't going to give him the answers he'd later claim as proof her son came through and communicated with him.

"He mixed up something. He messed it up." There was another pause. "He switched baking soda for baking powder." Morvan chuckled along with her, or along with her son, maybe both.

"They were interesting at best," Eileen confirmed. He couldn't have known about the pancakes. It was too much of a shot in the dark to be a guess. Her son really was talking to this man.

"He said you loved them. That's what he remembers most. It made him feel so good about himself. There was one left, and he couldn't swallow a single bite!" Morvan laughed again. "He's describing how awful they were, but he keeps repeating that you ate them and smiled."

Tears leaked from her eyes again. "Of course I did."

'My son made me breakfast. There's no way I wasn't eating it.'

"He loved baseball," Morvan continued. "He liked looking up in the stands and seeing his mom, cheering him on with pride."

"These are just a few of his memories he carries with him," Morvan continued. "He's always with you even when you can't feel him because he's not sure about the others."

"What do you mean the others?" Eileen asked ignoring his request she hold all questions to the end. It was sounding like he was wrapping things up anyway.

"Your son isn't the only spirit around us," he explained. "There are spirits everywhere whether you feel them or not. Some spirits keep more to themselves than others."

Eileen began fidgeting again. She was worried about Noah. The thought of him dealing with anything negative when she couldn't protect him ripped her heart out of her chest. She had let him down once in the worst possible way. There had to be something she could do to help him.

"Noah sounded young. How old is he?" Morvan asked, leaning back. The reading was officially over.

"Twelve," Eileen said. "Almost thirteen when the accident happened." Once again, she was thankful to hear Noah being spoken about in the present tense. Saying the words 'he died' had always been hard for her.

Morvan nodded and took a deep breath. "That makes sense. Being so young, of course seeing the other spirits is going to be off putting to him. They're not bothering him directly." He leaned back and slumped in his chair. "I'm afraid that's it for today. Connecting like this drains my energy, and it can be intense for those I'm speaking with as well. We both need to recharge."

It was hard to hide her disappointment. There was so much she wanted to say, to ask. She'd be back again and wondered how desperate Morvan would find it if she scheduled another session on her way out.

"There are ways to help protect his soul journey. Some patchouli would create an air of calm," Morvan told her.

"Can I schedule another session?" The words rambled together as they flew out of her mouth as quickly as she could say them. It was sounding like she was being dismissed to handle matters on her own, but she wanted help. "I would like to speak with my son again."

Morvan smiled softly at her. "We can. Certainly. It's preferred to wait two to four weeks between sessions. The longer the better because it's not an eternal rest if we're constantly interrupting them, is it?"

She nodded in agreement, but wanted to shout her objections at the top of her lungs. *'This is my son! He needs me as I need him. Even two weeks more is an eternity after how long I've already waited.'*

"I'm going to give you the address of a shop. I'm sure they'll have what you need there. You can also pick up a couple books on meditation and communicating with the other side. It helps to have a still mind. You have a lot going on, and it's quite jumbled. It's confusing even for you. It's like your brain is overworked and doesn't know how to take time off."

"You have to have quiet here," he said, pointing to his temple. "This has to be still in order for your son to communicate directly to you. It might not be as crystal clear as what I'm able to do, but you'll be able to sense him."

After scheduling an appointment for exactly two weeks later, she drove to Remus' shop. The session played in her mind on a constant loop during the drive, and she couldn't find any reason to doubt it had been real. The pancakes sealed it for her. What's more is the company he kept. Remus turned out to be just as genuine as Morvan. She could sense that right away too, and she held him close ever since. That friendship has proved to be most valuable to her in finding a way back for Noah.

Chapter Seven
Change of Clothes

Eileen opened her eyes and was greeted by the Egyptian eye of the bracelet that lay by her head. The smile on her face flowed freely for the first time in as long as she could remember. It was real. It hadn't been a dream.

The eye glared at her, and she pushed it watching the dagger appear. She pushed it again, and it retracted. *'An eye for an eye,'* she thought.

She didn't know if the Ancient Egyptians had a similar sentiment to the biblical quote, but she felt it was close. A life taken would bring back a life.

With a moan, she slowly stretched while her body voiced its complaints with various cracks and pops. The tile floor of the kitchen wasn't very forgiving on her old bones. It would be slow moving this morning, but it was the best place to sleep. The open doors of the dining room patio and the back porch created a pleasant draft through the kitchen. It was the coolest place in the house after the fire that burned for hours last night.

She pulled herself up and sat against the cabinets under the kitchen sink. Her stomach growled, but she wouldn't bother with looking for something to eat. Today was a very big day. Her nerves had kept her awake most of the night. If she even thought about eating for too long, she would be sick.

There was enough light coming into the room for her to realize it wasn't too early. That was good. The less time she had to worry about what must be done the less likely she would be to chicken out.

She continued to unfold her body and put her hands on the counter to pull herself up. Through the window, she could see the sun was higher than she expected. It was probably close to midday. She checked her phone for the time, but it was dead.

One pan sat on the island behind her with a little water left over. She took the overturned glass from the drainer and dipped it inside for a drink. Her body objected to every movement, but she needed to get going. There was a lot to do before nightfall.

She went to the bathroom, washed her face and brushed her teeth. There wasn't enough water to fill the tank, and she debated about leaving it. If everything went according to plan, she wouldn't stay here again. In the end, she couldn't let it be. It was true she was a shell of the person she used to be, but there were still a few standards she held on to. This was one of them.

This time she left the wagon. It was only one pan, and it would be quicker to carry it. She brought it back to the bathroom and dumped it into the tank, leaving just enough water in the pan to wash her hands.

Most of the clothes on the porch were dry. A few items were still damp in spots, but they were good enough. She quickly dressed, not bothering to go inside for privacy. There was no one around for miles. The clothing was stiff and wrinkled from the rudimentary way they had been washed. She folded the rest of her garments meticulously and packed them into her book bag.

She collected the pans from the house and placed them in the wagon, covering them with the tarp. The cleanup was almost complete. She hung her robe on the back of the bathroom door and made sure all the utensils were back in the sink.

It would seem pointless to most people that she even bothered to straighten up given how little there was left. Eventually the house would be sold. People would come to view it, and eyebrows would be raised. The one thing they wouldn't be able to say about her was that she was dirty. This was her home, and she had always maintained it. Even at her lowest, she couldn't leave a mess behind.

It took two trips to load her things in the back of the SUV. She walked up the steps for what was most likely the last time to lock the door. Looking down the hallway, she saw her son running to greet her like he always did when she came home. His arms were outstretched, and a smile spread from ear to ear. She bent down and reached out her arms to collect him, but right before she could, he disappeared.

Feeling her heart break all over again, she quickly reminded herself it'd be over soon. With any luck, they'd be reunited tonight. She pulled the door shut and locked all four locks.

In the driver's seat, she turned the key and checked her gas gauge. There was enough to get her into the city. She plugged the phone charger into the car lighter and tossed the phone on the passenger seat. Part of her knew she needed to get ahold of Remus as much as she dreaded it. The phone would have enough power when she got to the city for a call. She swore to herself that she would call him then unsure she'd follow through.

He had explicit instructions on what to do once she and Noah were safely away. She'd bring the bracelet to the house before they left. It would be returned to him then.

She pulled down the drive to the gate and felt a surge of newfound energy when she opened it. The adrenaline she felt would only continue to build. She pulled through the gate and left it open this time. Time would be of the essence once she made her move. If she had to come back to the house, she didn't want to deal with a heavy stubborn hunk of metal blocking her way.

Eileen sat parked outside a laundromat. The book bag in the back seat was now empty with her clothes neatly piled next to it. She was torn between hoping this wouldn't take long and hoping it worked at all.

The paintings had sold for a lot less than they're worth and less than she'd ever want to let them go for. They had been her dad's, and she treasured them.

When her father died, she collected an inheritance, but the family home, vacation properties, and all the contents went to his second wife. He was supposed to have updated his will, but he never got around to it. No one expects to die at the age of forty-six.

After his death, she went through lawyers and the courts. When that didn't work, she resorted to begging her step-mom. There were three small music boxes in her father's den that had belonged to her mother when she was a little girl. They were the only items in the house she wanted. Her step-mom wouldn't part with them, or at least took pleasure in denying Eileen from having them. Instead she gave her these paintings from her father's collection because they didn't mesh with her step-mom's taste.

She looked up and watched a car park in front of her. A couple got out and grabbed a laundry bag from the trunk. They wouldn't do.

It wasn't a total wash with the paintings. It did give her a few extra bucks she could take with her. She considered treating her son to a nice meal somewhere without having to touch the money set aside in the bag. He deserved it, but she wasn't sure if he'd be up for it. She wasn't sure what to expect at all.

Her stomach screamed at her again like it had been doing all day. She grabbed a few crackers from the sleeve laying on the seat next to her. It was the only thing she could bring herself to eat with her nerves on edge. Her hand grazed her phone as she pulled it away, reminding her she still hadn't called Remus.

Might as well make the call. It would be one way to pass the time. She picked it up and turned the power on for the first time that day then tossed it back on the seat. It would take a minute to fully come alive and update what she imagined would be a massive amount of notifications.

She took the bottle of water she had refilled at a gas station from the floorboard and took a swig, washing the salt from the crackers down her throat.

She glanced at her phone when she put it back. To her surprise, there were only two notifications. There was one missed call and one voice mail from Remus. She listened to it on speaker while keeping a close eye on the door to the laundromat.

"Hey, I'm not mad at you. I know you think I am, but I'm not. Please let me know you're okay, and *please* don't do anything rash. Wait until I've had a chance to decipher the hieroglyphics."

That was it.

A minivan with a loud exhaust pulled up behind her, and she looked in the rear view mirror. The driver was a significantly overweight middle aged woman. A teenage boy hopped out of the passenger side.

'This might work,' Eileen thought.

The boy went to the back of the van and made several trips unloading the baskets into the laundromat. He came back to his door, and the woman handed him something while barking out orders. Quarters, perhaps?

"Text me ten minutes before the dryers are done!" she yelled while the boy shut the door.

He went inside, and the woman pulled away.

Eileen straightened up in her seat, watching the boy's movements inside while trying not to be too obvious. There had to be something that would work if only he gave her the chance.

He pulled the baskets to an open row of machines. He arranged the detergents on top and bent down to begin loading the laundry. The boy stood up and looked around then grabbed the roll of quarters and darted to the bathroom in back.

'Perfect,' Eileen thought.

She grabbed the book bag from the back seat and darted inside. She passed the row of dryers behind where the boy's baskets sat on the floor until she found one with clothes resting inside. They didn't belong to any of the customers waiting. She'd been watching the building long enough to know that.

She opened the door and felt around the clothing, pretending to check if they were done. Her heart raced. She'd been living a pretty shabby life, but she had never resorted to anything close to this.

While she felt inside the dryer, she checked out what was inside the baskets. On one lay a pair of sweats, and the hood of a sweatshirt was hanging over the side of another one. They might do the trick. She just hoped they belong to the kid and not his mom. Even the kid's clothes would hang off her. There was no chance of getting the mom's clothes to stay in place.

She pretended to stuff the clothes from the dryer in her bag then turned around with a couple items in her hand that she not so accidentally dropped on the floor. The boy would be out of the bathroom any second. She needed to just do it. No one was paying any attention to her. An elderly woman dozed in the corner, and the young couple had their backs to her looking at the vending machines. She grabbed the sweatpants and sweatshirt from the baskets along with the clothes she dropped and shoved it all in her book bag as she left. When she walked around the side of her SUV, she could see the boy loading a machine. *'That was too close,'* she thought.

Eileen tossed the book bag across the car. It landed on the passenger seat and bounced to the floor. She climbed inside and was halfway down the block before buckling her seatbelt.

Two miles away in the business district, she pulled over. It wasn't exactly armed robbery, but theft wasn't in her nature. She looked around and checked her mirrors to make sure no one was coming after her. The pounding of her heart hit her chest hard enough to hurt and make her worry she might need a hospital visit. *'All this over a few articles of old clothing? How am I going to handle what's next?'*

She strained to reach the book bag, not thinking to unbuckle first. She opened it and pulled the hoodie, giving it a whiff. It actually didn't smell that bad. She did the same for the sweatpants, and they reeked. She'd just have to wear her own clothes underneath. Digging farther, she removed the clothes she had taken from the dryer. There was an old tank top that might fit and an old pair of men's boxer briefs. She scrunched up her nose and tossed them to the floor.

Checking around nervously once more, she reached into the back seat to get her clothing. She packed it all neatly back into her bag and carefully folded the tank top placing it with the clothes. Right or wrong, it was hers now.

The sweats stayed laying on the seat where they covered her cell phone that reminded her of her betrayal to Remus every time she looked at it. At least her laundry crime would serve more than one purpose.

Eileen pulled back on the road and made her way a few blocks to where the massive interstate bridge system that went around the city began. There at the bottom underneath all the immense tiers of concrete was a tent city. Most of the area's homeless found refuge there.

She drove as close as she could without driving through the heart of it. She avoided side streets and alleys where someone might take notice of her. It took a few laps until she found what she was looking for.

There was a secluded place to park that wouldn't be well lit at night. It wasn't in the best neighborhood, and she wouldn't want to leave the SUV unattended for long. Not that she would need to. From there, it would only take a minute to walk to the closest bridge. It should be easy enough to find a target.

Once she had a route planned out, she drove to the park where she used to take Noah after school. The playground equipment had been updated since they were last there.

Nothing in her life was the same anymore. She watched the other parents pushing their children in the swings and collecting them at the bottom of the slides, and she envied them. They still had their children. She prayed they never had to go through what she did.

Driving farther into the park near the walking trails, she pulled off in a spot well shaded by trees. She closed her eyes and sighed. The cell phone was fully charged. She was running out of excuses to not get ahold of him. She picked it up and sent him a text.

"I'm okay, and I won't," she lied. It was easier to not be truthful in a text than in person.

She cracked all the windows and turned the car off before climbing into the backseat. It wasn't exhaustion that made her go to sleep. It was not wanting to endure hours of waiting. When she wakes up, she would be closer to the moment that finally brings happiness back to her life.

Chapter Eight
I'm Sorry

Eileen woke to the sound of police sirens and sprang up in her seat to look out the tinted rear windows. The police cars whizzed right past her. Further down in the park is where lonely men went seeking male company. It looked like the cops were headed in that direction. Someone must have been doing something outside.

It took a few minutes for her heartrate to return to normal. It was illegal to sleep in your vehicle which had to be one of the dumbest laws she ever heard. It's your car, and you own it. Unless it's parked on private property, it shouldn't make a difference. If they had hassled her, it might have pushed off her plans for at least one more night.

She yawned and climbed back in the front seat. It was barely dusk. There was still a little time before the cover of nightfall would keep her hidden. It was enough time to drive her crazy if she let it.

She drove past a gas station not far from the bridge system and parked about a block away. Deep down she knew the cops would never trace anything back to her, but she didn't want her face showing up on a security camera this close just in case.

Taking her tote, she walked the edge of the road back to the station. She looked up and down the aisles at what they had available that her stomach might not reject. She settled on an individual tub of microwavable soup for $2.29.

'Highway robbery,' she thought. '*The only thing you actually pay for at a convenience store is the convenience.'*

Eileen took it to the back wall and microwaved it, digging through the bins. The clerk's voice from the front of the store yelled out, "Sorry. We're all out of spoons."

'Figures,' she sighed.

This way of life would be behind her she reminded herself. She removed it from the microwave, and put the lid on it. She wrapped it in paper towels to carry it to the counter to pay.

She walked back to her vehicle and waited for it to cool. The sun was still hanging on in the distance like it knew the longer it floated on the horizon, the better chance it had at saving her soul.

She sipped the broth. It was still too hot, and it could use some salt and pepper. She dug through the console between the seats. There were plenty of ketchup packets, but only one pepper. No salt. She poured it into the tub and stirred it with her finger.

She continued to sip on it slowly. So far so good. Her stomach was handling it well. She watched the cars pass by, not thinking about anything in particular. If she focused too long on anything, she might work up her nerves again. It was best to keep her mind clear.

After clearing away most of the broth, she brought the tub to her lips shaking some noodles into her mouth. They went down easily, but not for long. Seconds later she opened the driver's door and vomited into the street. Not even the threat of being hit was enough to make her risk getting sick on the interior. A bruised and battered sedan driving down the road honked at her as it swerved to avoid taking her door off as it passed.

She froze while the car barreled toward her, horn blaring, tires screeching as the driver tugged hard on the steering wheel resulting in a close call. Even though the car moved passed her without a scratch, her mind played the screeching sound of twisted metal as the car bent out of shape around a guard rail. It transported her to another time, another place.

When she collected herself, she closed the door and dug through all the nooks and crannies in her car until finally finding a towelette in her glove compartment. It was old, but it had retained most of its moisture. She used it to wipe off her face. Grabbing a water bottle from the floorboard, she swished the taste from her mouth. This time she checked for traffic before she opened the door to spit.

Her thoughts were transported back to the car accident three years ago that month. It was a fatal accident, and she didn't witness it. The one that had been mostly cleared by the time she made it to the scene. The one that haunted her waking life ever since, leaving her to find peace only in her dreams. The one she saw in her own imagination, playing on repeat, never giving her a moment's rest.

She closed her eyes and concentrated on her breathing. Slow, controlled, deep breaths in and out like the therapist taught her at the beginning. Nothing was going to stop her. It was time to make things right for what she had done.

It would be the wee hours of the morning before it would occur to her this near miss could place her close to the scene when the news broke, and the police asked the public for any information leading to an arrest. The driver of the car would likely remember the woman puking her guts out on the side of the road not two blocks from where it happened. It would be too late then. She would have already sold her soul in exchange for her son's.

Eileen drove to the intersection and turned left, parking at the end of the block on an unassuming side street. The alley ahead would take her straight to a smaller section of the tent city under the bridge. With any luck, she wouldn't have to go far because she needed to be able to make it back to her car quickly.

The top arc of the sun was barely hanging on. The sky was still filled with purple hues. In this part of the city where the interstate system loomed over the tall, brick buildings of yesterday, shadows stretched out encompassing the area for several blocks. Night time arrived earlier here.

She pulled her dishwater blonde hair back into a ponytail. The sweatshirt still lay on the seat where she had tossed it earlier. She quickly pulled it over her. It was a loose fit, but everything was anymore. The sweats were large enough to pull them on without taking off her cheap, worn out canvas shoes. The soles were completely rubbed down. There wouldn't be any shoe print patterns for detectives to go on.

The sweats would fall off her when she moved if she didn't hold them up. She dug through the tote until she found an old elastic. It was too stretched out for her hair, but had never been tossed. She gathered the sweats together at her waist and tied off the extra fabric with it, hoping it would hold.

A vision of her running back to her SUV while her sweats fell around her ankles flashed through her mind. It made her stomach flip, and she swallowed hard trying to keep down whatever was left that wanted to come up.

She took a look around. There was no one on the street

which didn't provide any comfort. There were eyes in all of these buildings: vagrants, drug addicts, prostitutes. The real questions were if they'd be willing to talk to the police, and if the police would put any stock into what they had to say.

The bracelet was still in the tote in an inside pocket, keeping it separate from the mess that was her oversized purse, her lifeline. She took it out and stuck it in the kangaroo pouch on the front of the sweatshirt unable to bring herself to look at it. Distancing herself right now was her only method to prevent chickening out. It was the only way she'd have the courage to keep her feet moving.

She pulled the hood over her head, covering part of her face, and climbed out of the vehicle. She locked the door with the key to avoid the beep-beep of the FOB alerting anyone of her presence who hadn't already noticed her. Cutting across the road at an angle, she headed toward the alley. She would stand out like a sore thumb. A woman getting out of a nice SUV in this neighborhood wearing oversized, worn out sweats alone was enough to catch people's eyes. Dressed like this on a hot July evening would make her even more conspicuous.

Eileen cut diagonally across the street at a slow trot. There was no traffic here. No need to rush. It was as if she was on autopilot trying to make her way down the small hill to do what she had to and back to her car as quickly as possible. She kept both hands in her pocket, clutching the bracelet tightly like she thought she might lose it. She traced her fingers repeatedly over the eye.

The bracelet was pointing to her left side, but she had to constantly double check. It had to be pointed in the correct direction, so when she pushed the eye, her hand would be clear of the blade. When she pulled the dagger from her pocket with her right hand, her dominant hand, it needed to be ready for action. The slightest mishap would make her lose her nerve. Everything had to play out perfectly.

As she approached the tent city, she saw three people on the far side under the overpass. They were walking slowly and muttering amongst themselves. They either weren't aware of her presence or didn't care about the person heading their way. She slowed her stride and walked along the edge of the disorganized make shift camp sites. Those three wouldn't do. She needed a loner. She walked along the mess of makeshift homes. There were a number of tarps and tents littered with piles of clothing and empty cans, and the occasional shopping cart for storage. The three in the distance had turned, walked up another alley and almost out of sight. It was looking like no one else was home at the moment.

She crossed the street and started walking past the tents on the far side of the bridge and was about to give up. She turned to make her way back to her vehicle, feeling a strange mixture of defeat and relief. Her determination rose up and motivated her to try somewhere else. If she didn't do this tonight, she might never have the nerve to make the attempt again.

That's when she heard it. The sound was hard to pinpoint because it was so faint. Her eyes scanned from one spot to the next. She didn't know who it was or where, but someone was snoring.

She zig-zagged around the junk that was strewn about everywhere trying to follow the sound. She side stepped around a pair of boots lying on the ground and almost didn't notice the legs they were attached to. The old man was laying on a pile of blankets next to a tarp strung over a cart on one side and pinned with a pile of cement blocks on the other.

Judging by his short white hair and the massive amount of wrinkles on his face, he had to be seventy at least. It made her feel better. Not because he had lived a long life, but because as weak as she had become, she could probably overtake him. With blinded focus, she knelt down beside him without thinking to glance around for witnesses.

She pressed the Egyptian eye on the bracelet and slowly pulled it from the pocket of the sweatshirt. "I'm sorry," she whispered. Her voice shook from her tears.

She jammed the dagger into the center of the man's throat. His eyes flew open, and he grabbed at her. Gurgling noises came from his mouth. She could barely see between the near darkness and the tears muddying her vision. Pulling hard to the left, she dragged the blade across his throat.

Within seconds, his grip on her loosened. His hands fell to his sides. The blood still poured from his neck, but his eyes were lifeless.

She jumped to her feet and quickly, almost running, headed in the direction of where she parked. Using the front of the sweatshirt, she wiped the blade of the dagger before retracting the blade and hiding it in the pocket again. The black material coupled with the black of night made it impossible for her to see how much of his blood she was wearing.

She was several yards up the alley when a woman's voice called out behind her. "Meg! Hey, Meg!"

Eileen ignored her and kept moving.

"Fine you old stuck up twat! I don't want to share my booze with you anyway!"

Eileen broke into a sprint, hoping whoever it was wouldn't come after her. Maybe this would be the break she needed when the police started asking questions. She hoped this woman would tell them she saw someone she knew leaving the area in a hurry.

Locking her door with the key hadn't been the smartest choice after all. It had to be unlocked that way too. Pressing the button on the fob would set off the alarm. She fumbled the keys in her hands trying to find the right one and dropped the keychain twice before finally getting the door open. She removed the bracelet and set it on the center console next to her.

She pulled away slowly going past the alley she had just left not glancing for one second in that direction, imagining a mob with pitchforks coming after her. Once the alley was safely behind her, she pulled off the sweatshirt with one arm and tossed it inside out into the backseat. A few blocks down, she made the turn onto a road that would bring her into a better part of the city, driving as cautiously as possible. Any of the street lights could be equipped to record, and it was becoming more common for businesses to have outside cameras.

After a few minutes, she made her way to a scenic route on the edge of the city. It would take her near the neighborhood where she lived, but that's not where she was headed. She chose this road for one and only one reason. There were no cameras. It was something she had bitterly learned through heartache. And if she was wrong, if the police were able to connect the dots, if somehow she became a suspect, they wouldn't find her. By then, she and her son would already be in Montenegro where they didn't extradite to the US. From there, the decision would be made where they would land permanently.

The homeless man she had murdered was the farthest thing from her mind as she approached the small bridge that went over Canyon Creek. This road used to be a favorite of hers. It was a quiet area where you could break up your busy city day by catching a glimpse of wildlife if you were lucky. It had been a long time since she drove it. The only reason why she went that route tonight was to escape any and all surveillance.

Thankfully there was no other traffic around when she made it to the bridge. She held her breath and shut her eyes tight when she drove across it, praying she didn't hit any ghosts. Her eyes watered by instinct, and she swallowed her sobs down hard once she made it to the other side.

On the other side of the bridge, she turned off and drove toward a more residential area of the city. There was no real rhyme or reason for the path she took. She was trying to stay as undetected as she could. Pulling into the first gas station she passed, she parked on the side near the restroom doors.

She shimmied the sweatpants off her legs and tossed them on top of the sweatshirt. She walked to the restroom hoping it was unlocked. The idea of having to go inside to ask for a key would take more nerve than she was capable of mustering. To her relief, the door opened when she turned the knob. She went inside and locked it behind her.

The stall provided some form of layered security that logically didn't make sense. Now that she was inside it, she didn't want to leave. She didn't want to rip off the tiers: stall, bathroom, and then the outside world.

It would draw as much attention if she stayed in the restroom too long as it would if she sped recklessly away from the murder. Finally, she left the stall and went to the row of sinks.

In the mirror, she noticed a few dark specks on her face. It was blood. It was the blood of the man whose life she took.

She threw up in the sink until there was nothing left and all that came out were dry heaves. She turned on the faucet, rinsing everything down the drain. Using her hand, she cupped some water into her mouth to rinse. When she looked back in the mirror again, she silently reprimanded herself. *'You're a murderer, Eileen.'*

After washing her hands and using paper towels to clean off her face, she grabbed another handful to wet down. There was no telling how much blood she tracked onto the seats. She went to the passenger side and opened the door. The driver's seat seemed clean, but she wiped everything down anyway even giving the bracelet a cleaning. It wouldn't completely erase any blood evidence, but at least it wouldn't be visible to the naked eye. It was the best she could do for now.

From under the seat, she grabbed a plastic store bag and began filling it. She tossed the used paper towels, the empty can of ravioli she brought from the house since she no longer had trash service, and the rest of the garbage in the car including the boxer briefs she stole and finally the sweatshirt and sweatpants. It was difficult, but she managed to cram everything into it and tie off the handles of the bag. She walked the few feet to the gas station's dumpster, tossing it inside. If there were cameras focused on her, it would simply look like she cleaned out her car.

Chapter Nine
Cemetery Watch

Eileen sat in the driver's seat of the car gripping the steering wheel to prevent her hands from shaking. She stared straight ahead at the wall of the gas station. The light underneath the eave of the roof flickered. Each time it did she thought she saw the Egyptian eye blink at her from between the seats. It was staring at her, reminding her of what she had done. Her own personal telltale heart wasn't going to let her relax.

Without looking at it, she threw it onto the passenger floorboard, so it couldn't watch her any longer. Then she tossed her tote bag on top, covering it completely. She knew if she moved her bag, she would find the eye was still staring up at her. The bag did little to shield her from the eye's stare which bore into her flesh.

In the distance, she could hear a siren. It grew closer and closer until it was upon her. She watched two police cars speeding past. They weren't after her, and they weren't headed in the direction of the bridge either. She gasped, not realizing she had been holding her breath, and a gush of air hit her lungs hard. It choked her, and she coughed for several seconds afterward.

She needed to go. She had wasted too much time as it was. For all she knew, her son was lost and looking for her. Not wanting to lead the police straight to him, she'd driven in circles and made a pit stop. Now she worried she delayed too long.

Leaving the gas station, she headed toward Woodhaven Cemetery. She drove past it slowly, peering through the wrought iron fence. There was no movement. She continued past the drive which was now barricaded. The cemetery closed at sun down. The gates were never locked on time. Whenever the caretaker got around to it was when it closed. Some nights the cemetery had still been accessible close to midnight. About a half mile down the road was a little opening in the trees just wide enough to pull her SUV into until it was parked safely out of view of the road. It was a spot she had discovered out of necessity one August.

Eileen walked to the other side of the vehicle and grabbed her tote without glancing at the bracelet. It was enough that she could feel it watching her. She went to the hatch and removed a couple tools, adding them to her tote.

It had been awhile, but she remembered the path she used to take up to the brick wall on the northern side. She chuckled when it came into view. The large rock she had rolled against it so long ago was still there. She put one foot on it and both hands on the edge of the wall then hefted herself on top.

On the other side, she walked straight toward her son's mausoleum. The idea of him being placed under ground had never sat well with her. Johnny had disagreed, but by then, he had given up arguing with her over anything. It was her money paying for it, and as long as his son had a proper service – which is something she had resisted at the beginning being unable to accept Noah's death – he didn't care so much where his son was laid to rest just so long as he *was* laid to rest.

The chain was still linked through the iron handles of the

two heavy cement doors and secured with a padlock. The night it was put in place was still vibrantly etched in her memory.

Eileen had been sleeping on the floor of the mausoleum near the pedestal where the burial vault resided like she had done every night for the better part of two weeks. She couldn't leave him. She wasn't ready to, not yet. Blessed in sweet dreams about her son who was still very much alive in them, she was rudely awakened when the doors burst open, and a light shown in her face.

"Here!" a man cried out. "Just as I told you. She's here."

Two policemen entered and told her to step outside. She panicked. She couldn't leave her son. What kind of a mom would she be if she abandoned her son when he was alone and frightened because he didn't know where he was or what had happened?

She threw herself over the burial vault, clinging as close as she could to him. They pried her fingers off and carried her out, setting her on the ground. They stood between her and her son, asking her to leave, and threatening to do things the hard way if she didn't. She dropped to her knees and bawled, watching one of the groundskeepers padlock the doors shut.

It hadn't been enough to keep her out of the cemetery at night. Those visits continued for well over a year. It only succeeded in keeping her out of her family's mausoleum. The third time the police were called to remove her from the cemetery after hours they took her down to the station and booked her. The charges were later dropped, but it was enough of a scare to stop her. If she was in jail, she wouldn't be able to continue her search for a way to bring her son back. She visited him only in the daytime after that, always telling him how sorry she was that she couldn't be there to keep him safe from the darkness anymore.

Eileen set her tote on the ground and pulled a set of bolt cutters out of it. They were heavy and awkward in her hands. It took her a minute to figure out how to unlatch them. The man at the hardware store had raised an eyebrow at her when she asked specific questions before purchasing them, but he assured her they'd cut through the chain she described. Whatever suspicious thoughts he had in his mind weren't enough to stop him from making the sale.

She positioned them around one of the links in the chain and pushed the handles together. To her surprise, they cut through the metal like a knife slicing butter. Whether it was because the blades were still sharp from never having been used or the chain was old and weak didn't matter. They worked.

The chain pulled through the handles of the doors easily, and she set it aside on the ground. The door creaked out a long groan when she pushed it open that echoed off the gravestones around her. Reaching back in her tote, she grabbed the crowbar to set to work on the burial vault.

Air slowly hissed out of it with each section she pried open. It wasn't until she loosened the third corner that the smell hit her. It wasn't that bad. It was an old, musty cellar stench. The worst was still ahead.

Eileen had to make several trips around it, weakening the seal in multiple places before she could finally budge it open. Even then, it was heavy enough that pushing it off was extremely difficult. She finally managed to move it over until it began to teeter on one side. With one last shove, it fell to the floor with a deafening bang that reverberated off the mausoleum walls.

After that, she opened the second door allowing more fresh air inside to help with the odor. She sat on the ground leaning her back against the small building, giving it some time to air out.

It had been almost two hours since she completed her mission under the bridge. She didn't know how much longer she had. All of the research her and Remus had found on the sacrificial dagger had either said less than a day or by morning. Remus speculated it would depend on how long the person had been deceased. Even if that were the case, it didn't give her an accurate window. The only thing she did have to go on is she didn't hear any noises coming from her son's coffin yet.

She picked up the crowbar and went back inside. Wedging it along the edge of the coffin, she stopped breathing through her nose. Everyone believed her to be crazy, but she wasn't stupid. It had been two years, eleven months, and twelve days since she lost her son. Once she broke this seal, it would reek. It wasn't a thought she dwelled on for long, but she knew her son's body was in a state of decay inside. By now, the decomposition should be reversing, but she didn't want to see it.

The crowbar worked its magic along the edge. She couldn't smell anything yet by only taking short gasps through her mouth, but her eyes watered. The stench hung around her and let itself be known.

She went to the back of the coffin and reached across it to lift it open. Grabbing the lip, she pulled it toward her. One side of the lid detached from the bottom when she did. She screamed and flung it back hard, shutting her eyes before running from the room.

Once she was safely outside, she bent over and took several deep breaths. The rancid smell of decay was able to reach her several feet from the doorway. She walked to the brick fence and rested where she could still see the doors, waiting for her son to walk through them.

Eileen stayed there well into the night, not realizing how tired she was until she woke up. Dawn was breaking, and the birds chirped their songs above her. She jumped to her feet and ran to the entrance of the mausoleum afraid to step inside.

She looked around the small room. It was empty except for the open burial vault in the center. Either her son's body was still laying in the coffin, or he was wandering somewhere lost and confused. She couldn't bring herself to look inside to see which it was.

When she shut the doors, she left them open a crack making it easy for her son to move them if he had not yet risen. She loosely linked the chain through making it look like it was locked. The chain would easily give and fall if the doors moved.

The bolt cutters were on the ground where she left them, and she put them in the tote. She looked around for the crowbar, but couldn't find it. She bit her lip and looked at the doors. It was still inside where she set it before opening the coffin. She lifted the tote and walked away. There was no more need for it anyway.

The cemetery entrance wasn't far, and she headed there first in case her son was looking for a way out. She couldn't find him anywhere. She wanted to keep looking for him. She didn't want to leave without him, but she knew the grounds workers would be here soon. If they saw her, there would be hell to pay.

Back at the wall, she used the decorative columns on the cemetery side for support to climb over. She got into her vehicle and turned the key. It was a little after six in the morning. She hit the steering wheel with both hands and screamed. There would be a lot of questions, a lot of scrutiny, police involvement, not to mention a media circus if her son roamed out and asked the wrong person for help.

There wasn't anything she could do. If she waited until the cemetery opened for the day and went inside, one of the groundskeepers would have to let her into the mausoleum. Even if she didn't ask to be allowed in, they all recognized her on sight after the past issues. Her picture probably hung in the office somewhere warning employees to look out for her. They would notice the chain had been cut and the morbid scene inside, and they would call the police. She would be arrested.

This was one part of the plan she hadn't thought through. Remus needed to hurry up and decipher the message. She needed to know before the workers began to arrive what to expect and when.

She plugged in her phone to charge then turned on the radio. She flipped through the stations, wanting to hear if there was any news on a homeless man found murdered. There was nothing, not even the smallest soundbite. All anyone had to talk about was Vietnam. It was on each station she flipped to.

'There must be some anniversary today, or a new memorial opening in the city,' she thought.

It had been a few minutes, so her phone should turn on by now. She flipped the radio off and checked. There were two messages from Remus.

The first asked how she was. "I haven't heard from you. Are

you alright?"

Followed by, "Made a little progress!"

She replied with, "I'm fine. What have you learned?"

The phone rang immediately. As much as she didn't want to talk to him, didn't want to talk to anyone, she knew she couldn't hide from him forever. "Hello," she said. "My phone doesn't have much charge," she added quickly.

"Where are you?" Remus asked.

"I'm in the car. Where do you think?"

"If either of us has a right to be mad, it's me not you," he pointed out.

"I'm not mad," she said. "My phone really will die soon, and you said you had news."

"I'll know for sure when I have the rest of them to use for context. This one suggests a familiarity. I think the sacrifice has to know Noah."

Eileen shut her eyes and tried to squeeze back her tears. Her lower lip quivered. She took a life for nothing.

"Still there?"

If she answered now, he'd hear the tremble in her voice. He'd figure out what she had done. She hung up and turned the phone off, leaving it on the charger. He could think her phone had died.

She carefully backed out onto the road and headed to her favorite diner. There was still time to catch the early bird special. The best thing she could do right now was not stray from her normal routine, not do anything that people might notice.

It wasn't long ago when she was the city's biggest advocate for the homeless. It was her platform. She worked hard to improve the shelters and rehabilitation services that would help them get back on their feet into a new home. It would also provide treatment for their addictions and mental health issues to aid them in living a normal life within society again.

There were fundraisers that she chaired and attended dozens more. She spoke at city council meetings on behalf of their plight. "The homeless are people too, and their fate could just as easily happen to any of us." She could hear her own words in her head that she had preached many times. Now here she was living a virtually vagrant lifestyle with the blood of a homeless man on her hands because when she discovered she would have to take a life to bring back her son, her first thought was no one would miss one of them.

Chapter Ten
Animated Theatrics

Her first visit to the Mystic Treasures shop almost left her feeling let down. This shop looked no different than the couple dozen other ones she had visited. They boasted books on every new age topic imaginable along with the basic supplies the authors recommended. It was one stop shopping for witchy culinary delights.

None of these books offered the answers she desperately needed to find. Some had their merits. A few of the meditations had been helpful, and the lemon lavender candles worked wonders on her stress. None of it brought Noah back or made her feel remotely close to him, not like sneaking into the cemetery after hours did.

Remus, the store owner, did his best to wow her with his books on communicating with the dead. She owned every one he sold and had read them from cover to cover so many times she knew the content better than his subpar sales attempts. Eileen needed more. She needed a miracle, but she didn't see a supply of those on the shelves.

"I'm sorry," she told him, searching over the tops of the displays for the entrance. "Morvan was under the impression you could offer something different."

"Morvan?" Remus asked in surprise. "Well, why didn't you say so?" The mischievous smile he flashed peaked her curiosity when he motioned at her to follow him. "What do you want to accomplish?" he asked. His voice was muffled since he was facing away from her.

"I don't know," she said. "I'm not really sure. Just something more than I've already tried."

"Of course you know," he said, walking behind the counter. "You can't change the past, but other than that, what do you want right now?"

Tears slipped from her eyes, and her lip trembled when she spoke. "More than anything, I just want to hug him one more time," she said. Her words came out broken in a voice barely above a whisper.

"One more time? Or every night from now on?"

She glanced at him then quickly looked away. She wasn't sure what he was on about, but it wasn't kind. Noah was gone. Hugging him wasn't an option, but Remus had asked. *'Of course I want to hug him every night for as long as I live! Wanting isn't the same as having. That is something out of reach.'*

Sensing her apprehension, he added, "I can help with whatever you'd like. Do you want to help him cross over?" Remus picked up a package of what looked like powdered herbs and scanned the candles displayed along the wall before pointing to one, "I've got what you need."

"Do you want to communicate with him? Clearly and on your own terms?" He picked up a small red velvety pouch with satin strings closing the top. "I have it."

"There's another group in town, recently relocated here. I don't know them as well as I should, but I've heard good things about them." Remus dug through a drawer and pulled out a pad of paper. He jotted a note on the top page and ripped it off. "They call themselves and what they do voodoo, but it sounds more akin to hoodoo. Is that a problem?"

Eileen shook her head no. She had no clue what he was talking about and had only heard the word hoodoo once in a movie. Voodoo was a New Orleans thing as far as she knew, and they were far from Louisiana. *'What does this group have to do with me?'*

He handed her a slip of paper with a phone number scrawled on it. "Make sure you give them my name. Remus."

She almost never went back to Mystic Treasures after her introduction to what those women called voodoo. It was an issue of trust. Remus had sent her there, clearly unaware of what was in store.

The group put on a good show. If nothing else, she could look at it as money well spent on theater. The entire back room of the house was decked out in candles and assorted dark décor. There were tapestries hung from the walls of people and scenes she wasn't familiar with which still haunted her dreams.

They lured her in with the promise of reanimation. They could bring Noah back. What they delivered was a confusing and absurd production that left her choking on her sobs as she ran to her car.

There were three women in the room when she arrived. Others went in and out, but Eileen didn't notice how full the room was becoming behind her until it was show time. They gathered everything they had asked her to bring: a picture of Noah, one of his favorite belongings, and personal items like his comb. And money, a large sum of cash.

Once everything was laid out, a man walked into the room wearing a headdress which covered his face and laid down on the table. Chanting and the sound of drums began behind her, and she turned, surprised to see the dozen or so others joining in the charade.

The man on the table lay perfectly still while the voices and drums grew steadily louder. It grew to a deafening pitch then stopped suddenly. His legs began to twitch, and his body shook like he was having a seizure before sitting abruptly upright. He stared directly at Eileen. Through his mask, she could see his cold black eyes staring back, and it terrified her.

He rose from the table and began to dance around the room. Shouts of excitement came from the extras whenever he approached them. When he made his way to Eileen, she froze.

"Talk to him," one of the women said.

"Here's your chance," added another.

'They can't seriously be implying this is Noah? That he is somehow in this grown man's body? He'd be cowered in the corner, hugging his knees to his chest, and crying if this were him.'

When she didn't speak, one of the crowd asked for her. "Are you alright dear child?"

The man didn't answer. He danced around Eileen in a way which made everyone cheer. Apparently his answer had been yes.

"Are you in a better place?" someone asked.

It was the same dance followed by the same cheers.

The room began to spin. The people swarmed her and faces came from every direction. "Ask him something! Do it now!" They were all yelling at her.

"Are you unhappy?" Someone else asked in her place.

The dance was different, but the delight it brought was the same. The answer was no.

She felt sick to her stomach. This wasn't what they promised. The woman she had been speaking with spoke of reanimation. That was the word she used repeatedly. Eileen had to look it up after their first conversation. It meant restore to life, to revive. This was nothing more than a pretend psychic pulling a scam with better set design.

The man's movements began to slow, and he headed to the table. "There's not much time," one woman told her, placing her arm around her. "What do you want to know?"

Eileen stiffened from the touch and tried not to scream.

"You want to know if your son loves his momma, don't you?"

The entire room was staring at her. The chanting had started up again, low and quiet. She nodded not knowing what else to do.

She looked away, squeezing her eyes shut. Whatever the man's response elicited another favorable reaction, but she didn't see it. Then it was over. The man lay still on the table, and the others left the room.

The three women were smiling at her, confident in the results they produced. "There child," one of them said, beaming a blinding smile. "Was it better than you expected?"

When she didn't answer, another woman said, "She's speechless!" She clapped her hands together before giving Eileen a hug.

Eileen let them draw their own conclusions. She couldn't say anything. If she opened her mouth to speak, the tears would come. She wasn't going to cry, not here, not around them. No one could console her, and the last people she wanted to try were the ones who dug up this wave of grief. If she had managed to start talking, it was hard to say what would've come out of her mouth. Underneath the sadness and grief, the pain and disappointment, an artic swell of anger was brewing.

They congratulated her like she had accomplished anything more than being duped. The man continued to lay motionless on the table which was more terrifying than when he danced around her.

She stayed only as long as necessary to collect the items she brought. Everything but the money of course. She wanted to chalk it up to a lesson learned, but it wasn't the first time someone took advantage of her broken heart. Deep down, she knew it wouldn't be the last time either.

One of them walked her to the door, and she ran to her car once she was alone. For hours, she drove around the city, crying, yelling to no one inside the car like a mad woman and screaming. There was no thought to where she was going except she wasn't ready to face the empty house yet.

When the car pulled up in front of Mystic Treasures, she was as surprised as she was angry. She slammed it into park and grabbed the key from the ignition. The car's lights flashed, and it beeped causing her to jump even though she had just pushed the lock button on the FOB out of habit. She had kept everything locked inside around the people who took her for a fool, but somehow she felt it was okay to place the blame on Remus. He's the one who sent her there.

The "Closed" sign was hanging on the door, but there were lights on in the back. She wasn't sure if he was still around. The shop hours said he closed at nine, but she didn't know what time it was. Her watch wasn't on her wrist. Another in a long list of surprises tonight. Sometimes she remembered it, but it was becoming less likely for her to put it on before she left the house. Her phone was in her purse in the car.

Eileen pounded on the door. There was nothing. No movement anywhere in the store. She pounded on it again hard enough she thought it quite possible the glass might shatter. "Remus!" she screamed over and over.

Finally, she saw him, saw a figure anyway, and watched him maneuver through the shelves of books and other displays. When he reached the door, she saw a flash of recognition in his eyes. He lifted his hand to the lock, but hesitated.

"You did this!" she screamed at him.

He unlocked the door and opened it, catching her in his arms when she fell inside. "You did this," she repeated, sobbing into his shoulder while he held her.

Eileen didn't stop crying until there were no more tears left to shed. Remus brought her to the back of the store and led her up the stairs to his apartment. They sat in the kitchen until the sun came up talking about Noah over coffee. He didn't say much, but let her ramble away without complaint.

"I am truly sorry," he squeezed out before the yawn took over his ability to talk. The dim light of day break was coming through the small window over the sink. "I told you I didn't know much about them, but I should've vetted them more before sending anyone to that mockery."

She half shrugged and stared out the window. There wasn't much to see except a gray and dismal morning and the back of the brick building his window faced. If she leaned over a little she could see a window on the building. It looked like an apartment, and she was curious about the people who lived there. She found all people fascinating. It was like the living went on around her, experiencing their normal day to day, while she was stuck in limbo.

"This is what you want? To bring him back to life?" he asked her.

They were both tired. The conversation was turning into nonsense and wishful thinking.

"It's not possible," she admitted out loud. It was the first time she allowed herself to speak the words into existence, but she had always known it was true. Dead is dead. It's exact and final. Her son had been gone almost a year. Any hope of saving him ended that night the doctor walked into the waiting room.

"Maybe," he said. "But what if it could be done?"

The tears were returning. She must have drank enough coffee to begin building a reserve. They'd be more bitter this time, stinging when they released and piercing her tongue if they made it to her mouth. Remus had seen enough of her heartache. She'd hold them in until she returned home.

"It's getting late," she said, pushing away from the table. "Or rather, it's getting early." She actually laughed at her joke. It was a soft chuckle, and the smile faded as soon as she felt it stretch her lips. Still, it felt good while it lasted.

"Many cultures have a history steeped in bringing the dead to life," he pointed out quickly.

"Yes, like hoodoo?" She stood up and grabbed her keys. For the first time, she realized her purse had been sitting on the passenger seat all night, and she hoped it was still there when she got to her car. In a softer voice, she added, "Their interpretation of reanimation isn't necessarily the one I'd want. Just like with those people last night."

She made her way to the stairs she knew would lead her to the store not giving Remus any choice except to follow.

"You're right," he said. "But that doesn't mean there isn't a way."

Eileen weaved through the store and stopped at the door. There was enough light to see her SUV parked right across from it. The windows all looked intact. She had caught a break for a change and wouldn't have to worry about replacing her driver's license. "I can't handle more of this," she told him. "I'd be happy simply communicating with him."

Remus nodded like he understood. "Let me check into it then. It might never lead to anything. Leave me your number, will you? In case I find something useful."

Whether it was from exhaustion or being willing to do anything to leave, Eileen told him her number which he scrawled on his hand. She hadn't expected to hear from him for a while, if at all. The almost daily text messages updating her on what he was checking into and making sure she was alright were annoying at first, but soon became the only thing binding her to sanity.

Chapter Eleven

Vietnam

It had been three days since the bridge incident as Eileen was referring to it in her mind. She felt like a prisoner in her own home. Her one and only morning of trying to act normal didn't go very well. Three people in the diner had been discussing what happened in Vietnam. It messed with her mind. It was too surreal for her to try to understand in the context of present events. Vietnam had happened over forty years ago. It shouldn't be such a hot topic now without an important anniversary or current memorial being held.

Eileen always measured time by the most intense event she'd experienced. There was one life before she lost Noah. It was so dramatically distorted from the way she existed now it was hard to believe it had ever been real. His death sent her into a parallel world where everything was different even though the only thing changed was his absence. Her visit to tent city shifted the paradigm again. All of the talk about Vietnam since then confirmed this, but it wasn't reassuring. It caused her to freak out even more. Her reality had been hanging by a thread for a long time, but taking a man's life caused it to snap. She was gripping the edge as tight as she could manage, but her fingers were slipping.

Every person who looked at her was recognizing her from a wanted poster that didn't exist. Every whispered conversation was about how she looked like the person police suspected of murder. The voices swirled round and round inside her mind as bits and pieces she could see, like cartoon birds after someone received a whack to the head. It made her dizzy as she tried to follow them. Her anxiety convinced her that every person she saw was readying to turn her in for a reward. The fear it caused her made her more awkward, louder, more likely to say or do the wrong thing, and all around more noticeable than usual.

She bought a bottle of bleach, hydrogen peroxide and a case of instant noodles then holed herself up in her home. If she thought it wouldn't ruin it, she would've soaked the bracelet in hydrogen peroxide. Instead, she dipped her toothbrush in the bottle and scrubbed it several times a day. She scrubbed her hands and face with the bleach, being careful to avoid her eyes. A watered down solution of it was used to wipe down the seats of her vehicle without a care if she stained them.

The kitchen was her cell. She slept on the cold tile floors and spent most of her days hiding between the cabinets and the island only venturing out back for water at night. Twice a day, when she woke up and before bed, she'd idle her engine to charge her phone long enough to see if there was anything from Remus. There hadn't been until this morning. He sent a link to a news article asking in all caps, "WAS THIS YOU?"

The article, if it was long enough to call it that, was two small paragraphs about the discovery of a murdered homeless man in the city. At this time, it hadn't been determined how long he had been dead before his body was discovered. It said the police had no suspects. It could be a red herring. Something aimed to make her feel comfortable enough to come out of hiding where she could be found. If they knew her name, they would be able to find her address. If they only knew her face, this would be the safest place to stay.

She lied to Remus again telling him, "Of course not." It was becoming easier to distance herself from reality especially when she didn't have to look someone in the eye to do it.

That night there was another message. "Call me."

Eileen stared out her windshield, shaking her leg, and pinching her lip between her thumb and forefinger under the pretense of waiting for her phone to charge. The truth was she dreaded making the call, dreaded hearing that he knew what she did.

She had sent a reply asking what was going on, but he only said he'd tell her when she called. It could be news of the bracelet, but her anxiety insisted otherwise. Both of her legs began to shake hard enough to rock her car.

"Ugh," she groaned out loud, rubbing her temples. *Do it, and get it over with,'* she thought. She dialed his number preparing to hang up before he answered.

"Hey," Remus connected before the end of the first ring. "I wondered if I was going to hear from you."

"I'm here," she told him.

"And where is that?"

"At the house."

Remus didn't say anything right away. He knew how much she hated being there with the memories that haunted her. "Well, I just wanted to give you an update. I am certain now there has to be some form of familiarity. I think the person who dies by the dagger may have to know the person who is coming back."

"What do you mean?"

"It's too early to say. I don't know if they have to be a willing sacrifice, or if the person who comes back is just someone they know, someone they're thinking about maybe."

This news wasn't boding well for her. The only other person who had a connection to her son was her ex-husband. If he suddenly wound up mysteriously murdered, the focus would definitely be on her. The same went for his new wife. The cops would be at her door before the blood dried if anything happened to Meredith. The record of their assorted public, and quite undignified, scenes in the early days after Noah's death would tip the police force off immediately.

"How are you holding up?" Remus asked.

"I'm at my wits end," she said, staring at nothing out the window. Her wits ended long before the dagger was located, but telling him she was too far gone to be saved wasn't going to work out in her favor either.

"I know. I'm trying. You have to believe me. I'm working on this as hard as I can."

Eileen didn't doubt that. They had met when a gifted psychic recommended him, giving her the name of Remus's shop. They became close after that awful voodoo ritual sham. They tracked down a few leads into ancient mysticism and witchcraft before landing on an old document that mentioned the dagger. During the close to two years he helped her search, they became friends. He wanted this for her almost as much as she wanted it for herself.

"Sit tight. It's a hard task to accomplish, but remember, we're in this together. I'll even drive the getaway car."

She wanted to laugh at his old joke, but she couldn't even manage a smile.

"Hey! While I got you," Remus went on, "have you heard about that guy they found in Vietnam?"

With all she had experienced in her life, it still amazed her at how cruel some people could be. A young American punk wandered into a town in Vietnam claiming to be a soldier whose plane was shot down in 1973. Even assuming its true, assuming he's been a prisoner of war for all those years who finally managed to escape, he'd be an old man by now.

According to Remus, this kid didn't look a day over the age of nineteen. When she thought about all the unnecessary trauma this kid was causing people, it angered her. All of the soldiers who lived through it were now subjected to hearing this. All of the families who lost loved ones over there, especially the ones who never learned of their fate, were forced to grieve again.

He had done his research beforehand. The name he had given was a soldier who had been declared missing in action after his helicopter went down. It was impossible that he was the same person. The jerk was refusing a DNA test, claiming the doctors were trying to experiment on him. The American government was intervening, trying to bring him back to the states. Then they could court order a psychological evaluation as well as medical testing to determine his real identity.

'No wonder Vietnam was all over the news,' she thought. There was something deep seeded about this kid. Whether it was an untreated mental health issue which could be managed with proper care or he was a psychopath was the question.

It was easy to forget other people had problems too. She could, and would, use the crutch of being wrapped up in her own issues if anyone ever broached the subject with her. The truth was she had always been this way. Growing up with money made it easy to discount what other people went through. It wasn't like she was oblivious to the plight of others in the world. None of it ever hit close enough to home to make it real. Child abuse or addictions like drugs and gambling only happened in impoverished areas. These weren't concerns of the everyday person.

'It's easy to be self-centered when your life was sheltered. I never had to learn empathy.'

Eileen had never felt more naïve as she had when she walked into the Country Club bathroom and saw Abigail dipping into a vial of cocaine. This was a woman she had been playing tennis with for years but had no idea about this side of her.

"Just need a quick pick me up," Abigail laughed. She lifted a tiny spoon to her nose right in front of her. Like it was no big deal. It wasn't a secret.

She struggled with what to do with the information for a long time. Did she stage an intervention? Inform Abigail's husband? Call the police? This was unchartered territory for her. Without an answer, she asked Johnny about it. He laughed at her like her lack of life experience was comical. "Don't worry about it," he said, shaking his head. "Half the club does it. The other half does worse."

Eileen never looked at her former friend the same way again. When the members of their mutual clubs applauded Abigail for her organizational skills, her enthusiastic nature, the seemingly endless amounts of energy she had to pour into a project, Eileen would silently stew over the truth.

Even when she first lost Noah, she never stopped to think about the other mothers before her who had to bury a child. This was her pain. It was an agonizing torture she endured alone. There was no one who could possibly understand what she was going through. Perhaps if she had reached out with these support groups, really given them a chance, reached out to some of these other women who had experienced the loss of a child, she wouldn't be in her kitchen scrubbing an ancient bracelet for at least the hundredth time in the last three days.

With all of this, she could never do something as cruel as what this young punk was trying to pull overseas. The anguish it had to stir up for all those who lost a loved one in that war was heartbreaking. She hoped every charge possible was thrown at him and a few new ones if necessary.

'Someone who knows Noah.' The thought resurfaced while she rinsed out her toothbrush.

The rolodex of names from her other life flipped through her mind. Teachers. Coaches. Parents of friends. One of Landon's parents was a brief possibility. They should have never allowed Noah to leave their house that late on his own, riding his bike in the dark.

It was unfair to Landon. While she hadn't kept in contact with the family, the last time she spoke with his mom she learned he was in therapy. He felt guilty for the argument he had with Noah that evening. Eileen didn't want to add to what this boy was going through by taking one of his parents away too.

She targeted the homeless man because she thought no one would miss him, but the words of the woman who followed her out of the tent city haunted her. She awoke from nightmares by the sound of, "Meg! Hey, Meg!"

People like Eileen wouldn't notice the death of a homeless man. There was clearly a sense of community within the homeless population. They would mourn their own. Not only that, but they would now live in fear of someone attacking them while they slept.

The life she lived before included working for different organizations on projects like helping the homeless. She was the ringleader behind raising money for a new day center. It was touted as a saving grace for them to have a place to go, to interact, hang out, and have the semblance of a normal life. Once it was all said and done and the money was raised, she barely followed the details of the construction. She was only present for the ribbon cutting ceremony because she had been an integral part of it.

After that, it was out of sight, out of mind. She didn't stick around to see how few people actually used it. There was no consideration of whether it was money well spent or something which would be a burden on the city from here on out with the upkeep and maintenance required to run it. The only thing that ever mattered to her was the recognition she received for doing her part.

If she had truly wanted to help the homeless, she could've raised money for free counseling to treat mental health and substance abuse issues. She could put them into contact with advisors volunteering their time who would help them find employment. The money could've gone to warmer clothing, blankets, and socks. A soup kitchen which would give them a box containing a hot meal to take with them when they didn't pass the breathalyzer test to be allowed inside could've made a difference. The things the homeless really needed were overlooked, but she was still touted as a savior to them for the work she had selflessly done.

'Meg! Hey, Meg!'

It made her realize everyone held the possibility of being loved and missed. No matter whose life she took there would likely be somebody who'd be hurt. The next person she targeted needed to be someone whose death would make the world a better place. It had to be someone who the majority of people would be happy to hear had died.

'If only that Vietnam liar was already in the states,' she thought.

Chapter Twelve
Paper Cuts

On the fourth morning after the bridge incident, Eileen woke up motivated and got ready with a plan in mind. Remus had said the sacrifice had to be familiar with her son. It only left her two initial options. Either she murder her ex-husband or a parent of one of Noah's friends while telling them the reason she was killing them to help ensure he came back to life. Either of those options would leave the detectives straight to her especially if it was discovered Noah was once again among the living. Or, she make someone familiar with her son before they died.

The thoughts had plagued her most of the night keeping her awake. On the one hand, the wise thing to do would be to wait and have Remus decipher the hieroglyphics. Let him figure out exactly what needs to be done for this to work. She even considered there might be some phrase or chant that needed to be recited while the dagger was being used.

She was out of patience. It had been spent right along with her fortune. Now, she was so close. The bracelet that concealed the dagger was in her hands.

There was another far more pressing issue for her to not want to wait. Because she had jumped the gun, the mausoleum and the coffin where her son had been entombed were open. It was only a matter of time before someone gave that building a closer look and noticed the chain was broken.

Her fingerprints were all over it. Plus there was the crowbar she had left inside. She couldn't go back, not while her son's lifeless body remained inside visible to anyone who entered.

It was supposed to be easy. No, nothing about committing murder was easy. It had, however, been simple. Sacrifice a life. That was the hardest part. It was something that until she did it she wasn't certain she was capable of doing. A life had to be sacrificed, and she chose a homeless person because she thought the investigation would be weak. She thought she could get away with it.

Sacrifice a life. Collect her son. Hop on a plane. It seemed so simple when she detached herself from it.

Three entire and very long days had passed for her to think about what she had done. The hysteria she was feeling was harder to keep buried. Random moments turned into outbreaks of panic and fear, remorse and regret. These feelings would have surfaced even if it had worked. She'd have episodes in front of her son in a country foreign to both of them making it worse, but at least she'd have Noah. He would be a reminder of why it was worth it.

Nothing eased what she was going through. It was a random, senseless act, and it would affect people even if she didn't witness the aftermath. She had committed murder with nothing to show for it, nothing gained. It meant she was no better than those behind bars paying for their crimes.

Deep down, she understood it was wrong even if it brought her son back. It was just easier to accept why she sold her soul if it had been for more than practice.

Everything had gone wrong. She had been seen in the homeless community although she didn't know how good a view the woman managed to get of her, or if the woman had paid attention to the vehicle that drove away a few minutes later.

She broke into the mausoleum and opened her son's coffin for him to easily climb out. That was four nights ago. Thankfully nobody seemed interested in visiting their dead. If the deceased were properly looked after, someone would've noticed the stench being emitted from the mausoleum by now.

Waiting for Remus was no longer an option. That's what she should've done from the start. There wasn't any time left to waste. It could come at any moment. The cops could bear down on her home because an eye witness caught the license plate on her SUV driving away from the bridge that night. Someone at the cemetery could discover the disturbed coffin. Even without her history at the cemetery, she would be one of the first stops the police made as Noah's mother, but given their previous interactions, she would be a prime suspect.

Eileen got dressed in one of the nicest outfits she owned. It was from the duffel bag. She hadn't wanted to get into those clothes yet, but she told herself it would be alright. Tonight was the night she would take her son to depart on a new life together. It was only appropriate she'd be dressed in something other than rags when they saw each other again.

When she stood in front of her bathroom mirror, it was both hard to recognize the shell of the woman staring back at her and hard not to see how far she'd fallen. The clothing hung off her like a teenager who raided her older sister's closet. It made her look poor, unkempt, and rather less attractive than the bony joints and hollowed cheeks already did.

It could work to her favor. She pulled her hair into a ponytail. It was the lazy woman's hair-do. This style was reserved for worn out middle class mothers existing on exhaustion, flavored mixed caffeine drinks barely resembling or containing the coffee their body's craved, and shattered dreams of what they had planned to accomplish in life. It was worn by women who wanted to keep their hair out of their face while they exercised and women who had given up on themselves. This was the hairstyle she'd preferred for a long time. There were too many important matters to focus on to waste a valuable second on her hair.

The look was perfect. There was a time she hated to see the ponytail looking back at her, but she had gotten used to seeing it. The hanging hair was a permanent extension of herself. After some time, she rarely looked at the woman in the reflection, unable to face the person she'd become. Today she liked the woman looking back at her. It wasn't someone she'd want to meet or befriend, but if anyone was watching out for her as a suspect in the murder she committed, they wouldn't look twice at this image.

Using her phone, she created a word document. She found her son's last little league photo taken a couple months before he died. It was one of her favorites. His smile beamed bright enough to light even the darkest soul. This was the face she was fighting to bring back. He deserved a second chance.

Noah loved baseball. He loved playing third base. He was his team's last chance before a runner headed for home, and he played the position with pride, like it was an honor. He had spent hours in the backyard with the pitching machine his dad had bought him, improving his swing to be one of the better batters in the league.

'His dad,' she scoffed. *'His dad probably wasn't aware their*

son played ball until the second season.' Johnny ignored all the notes and marks on the calendar regarding practices and games. The league pictures had been added to the carefully chosen framed family photos for months before he saw there was something new.

It was Eileen who had mentioned the pitching machine one night in a conversation Johnny half ignored. She got into bed worriedly venting about how Noah was smaller than most of his teammates. He couldn't keep up with them when he ran. A pitching machine would help improve his eye where he could compete with the other boys if not blow them away.

Less than a week later, his dad brought one home with him after work. The best and newest model of pitching machine which was bought from his wife's account.

"I don't even know where the idea came from," Johnny had laughed. "It just hit me. A pitching machine! What else could be better to help you improve?" he told Noah.

Later that night, he brought it up again to Eileen. "If only there were more hours in a day, I'd have the time to work with him on the fundamentals. I mean it's not like you would be able to teach him anything about baseball."

It irritated Eileen, but she'd made the decision when Noah was a baby she'd never do or say anything to discount his opinion of his father. *'Maybe if you weren't trying to juggle so many women, you'd have the time,'* she thought. Her cheeks were hot and felt fiery red, but Johnny didn't say anything. He paid less attention to his wife than he did his son. An argument would carry down the hall and Noah would overhear, probably sneaking toward their room out of curiosity to listen better. Fighting with him over something so unimportant wasn't worth it. She liked the idea of Noah having one, and now he did. That's what mattered.

Noah couldn't stop talking about it for weeks. It was all he wanted to do. When he was forced to come inside to eat or go to bed, he raved on and on. He was always sure to mention how great his dad was for buying it for him. It hurt how everything she did was overlooked. Not entirely, but enough to bother her. She received thank you's and I love you's. Some were filled with excitement and others were routine. Johnny would swoop in once or twice a year with a grand gesture at Eileen's expense and be the hero for months.

Eileen always had to remind herself it was a waiting game. *'As Noah grows up, he'll see for himself who was really there for him. He'll figure it out.'*

Remembering how she used to suffer in silence put a lump in her throat and a wail of grief on her lips. Noah wasn't given the chance to grow up. It was stolen from him by an entitled washed-up has-been. *'But I'm going to bring him back.'*

"Who's the hero now, Johnny?" she asked her phone. "You wouldn't have the guts to do what your son needs now if you even think about him at all in your new life."

The document she had created looked perfect. It was almost truthful and a sinful lie in one. Noah's face grinned at her from her phone, and brought a kiss to it with her finger. "It won't be much longer. I promise."

Making her way to the small shop on Sixth Avenue, she drove as carefully as she could. The last thing she needed was a routine traffic stop where she might match the description of a person of interest. The radio blared news of the young man in Vietnam. It was everywhere, and she couldn't get away from the story with any of the presets programmed. If one station was playing a song or had a commercial break when she landed on it, Vietnam would be the next topic when it ended. The US Government was doing everything necessary to bring the young man home. It was a growing concern because the man was being viewed by foreign governments as some kind of a plant to stir up tensions, and it was believed his life might very well be in danger.

'*Serves him right for pulling a stunt like that,*' Eileen thought, turning the radio off because she was tired of listening to it. Something else newsworthy needed to happen soon, so this story could be laid to rest.

She pulled into the parking lot of Paper Cuts shortly after they opened at ten. It was a one stop shop for all your printing, copying, and laminating needs. She had used them many times during her fundraising days for fliers and pamphlets. Staying local and supporting small business won her more accolades. No one had a clue she chose them because their prices were cheaper. She had never been the errand girl who had to pick up the order. They wouldn't recognize her.

The college aged kid working the counter didn't look up when she walked through the door. "Welcome to Paper Cuts. May I help you?"

"I need to print a document from my phone," she said.

He pointed to a row of computers along one wall without taking his eyes off the comic book he was reading.

She took the charger from her tote and removed the base, plugging her phone into the computer. In a minute, the document appeared in front of her on the screen. It was an eight by ten page with the word "MISSING" prominently displayed in all caps on top above the picture of her son. The name "Noah McBride" was written in smaller letters underneath it, but the rest of the details were fake. "If you have seen this boy, please contact Karla," followed by a phone number she had made up.

"Where does this print to?" she asked loud enough to get the kid's attention.

He straightened up and answered, "Back here." He pointed to a large office printer behind him.

'He's going to ask questions,' she thought.

"Just print one. Any additional copies we'll do on the floor," he said, pointing to a cluster of computers positioned on small tables in a circle near the center of the store.

Against her better judgement, she pressed print. She didn't know where else to go besides the library. Their printers were behind the desk as well.

She grabbed her stuff and walked up to the counter. The employee begrudgingly retrieved her paper from the printer. It was obvious he didn't enjoy having his heavy reading interrupted by his job.

When he looked at it, he softened. "I'm so sorry," he told her.

Eileen nodded, and asked, "How much?"

"You just... want... the one?" he asked.

"Oh," she stumbled, trying to come up with an explanation on the spot. "It's not... He's not... He goes to my son's school. I thought I'd just keep a copy in my car. You know? In case I saw him."

The clerk didn't look like he believed her, but he slid the paper across the counter and rang her up. "That'll be $1.63." he told her.

'For one color copy!' Eileen thought. *'No wonder they stay in business. Cheaper or not, it's still ridiculous.'*

She paid and took the page with her, heading to the address she had looked up before she left the house. She wasn't going to make a move in broad daylight, but she wanted to find the place, wanted to look for exit routes while there was still plenty of light to see by. When she came up with the idea of how to choose who was next, there was one person who stood out in her mind. His name had been plastered over the local news, even going national at least once.

And, the best part was no one would miss him. If anything, she'd be considered a hero who had performed a great public service for the city.

Chapter Thirteen
Have You Seen This Boy?

The home of Chuck Rogers was nicer than she expected, nicer than he deserved. It sat in what used to be a quiet residential area outside of the city, but now the city was expanding to meet it. The house was an unassuming one story with an enclosed front porch giving him privacy he didn't need, but that privacy would be to her benefit.

Two blocks away was a large twenty-four hour supermarket that anchored a strip mall. Eileen pulled into the parking lot to think. With the side streets, there were multiple routes she could take to and from Rogers' house. As she sat in the lot, she watched many people leave their cars in one area while they walked to a different store. No one would pay her much mind if she used the parking lot to hide her vehicle in plain sight later on that evening.

She had hours to kill until then. With nowhere better to go, she went into the store to take advantage of the free air conditioning. She walked up and down each aisle, studying the products, doing her best to fit in as a conscientious shopper.

There was a small stationary section, and she eyed the new release books. There was one aimed more for high schoolers with a dragon and an elf on the cover. It was right up her son's alley. He loved everything fantasy. She put it in the cart thinking he might like something to keep him occupied on the long flight ahead.

After spending over an hour walking every inch of the

place, she added a package of baby wipes to clean up without having to boil water at the house to bathe. She also treated herself to a deli sandwich. Her body wouldn't know what to do with that heavy a meal.

Back in the car, she saw it was barely noon. The day was going to drag. She ate her sandwich slowly, unable to finish it. She wrapped it back up and tucked it underneath the seat near the floor vents hoping it would stay fresh for later. Even if it didn't, she knew she would probably eat it anyway.

She needed something to wear tonight, but didn't feel like attempting another laundromat heist. There was a thrift shop nearby. She went there and purchased an oversized windbreaker. It would be enough to protect her clothes she hoped.

In the last few years, she discovered dozens of places in the city where it was safe to park while she slept. She considered taking a nap to make the evening come quicker again, but didn't want to risk waking up to a police man rapping on her window. In the depths of her soul, she knew her description was out there. It was being repeated over police radios, reported on news channels she couldn't watch, and announced on the radio stations she tried to avoid. The best option was to go home and count the tiles on the kitchen floor like she had done a thousand times since the accident.

'*Not for much longer,*' she convinced herself on the drive home.

Eileen didn't want to nap on the kitchen floor again. It would be too hard, and she'd wake up too stiff for what she had to do. Instead, she pulled up to her house, rolled down the windows and slept in the backseat. When she woke up, it was dark, and the crickets chirped out a chorus to each other wondering what this crazy woman was doing.

She opened the rear door and stepped outside. The urge to use her bathroom was hitting hard, but she didn't feel like messing with the locks. She walked to the overgrown bushes near the house and hid between two of them to do her business. There was no one around for miles, but she hadn't yet completely lost her sense of propriety.

Back in the front seat, she turned the key. It was half past ten. She had been out a lot longer than she expected. She didn't know much about Chuck Rogers besides his past. It was unlikely, but he may keep early hours that would already have him in bed asleep. He could work third shift and be gone by the time she arrived at his house.

If she didn't catch him tonight, she could try again tomorrow. The pesky worries of her mind wouldn't let her stay so calm. There was still the possibility her son's disturbed coffin would be discovered. She might not have another day.

She drove to the supermarket near Rogers' house not caring what route she took. Going to a grocery store wasn't a crime. Rogers, however, would be well versed in what was and was not criminal. He was a monster who deserved to rot in hell for what he had done even if the police had never been able to prove anything.

Chuck Rogers was reputed to be a child molester. The first victim had lived next door to his mother's house. Little Emma had grown up familiar with him as he visited a lot. She was the only child of a single mom, so Chuck helped out where he could. They had always considered him a friendly neighbor even though he didn't live there. He fixed the brakes on her bike, put air in her tires, and even helped her mom out with a leaky faucet once. It seemed like he only had their best interest at heart.

When Emma went missing, the police ruled him out as a suspect. He had been at work that day. If Emma's mom had known that her daughter had actually left the house late the night before and wasn't there that morning to leave for school like she had believed, the police would've realized that Rogers had opportunity.

Emma had never been found. It happened over four years ago, but there were never any solid leads to solve the case. Three more young girls went missing in the year following from neighboring communities. Their bodies had all been discovered along the banks of Canyon Creek. They had suffered unimaginable sexual torture before their deaths. Rogers had been looked at as a suspect, but there was only one case where there was anything substantial to pin it on him.

He walked on a technicality. Four children. Four horrid nightmares. No justice. They were able to convict him on obstruction of justice, and the judge gave him the harshest punishment the law allowed. He was out after serving a little over a year without his name on a sex offender list to warn others.

That wouldn't be the case for long. Eileen was about to see to it that he never harmed another child.

She pulled into the supermarket lot and parked near the far end. It was closest to the street she'd use to make her way back. She walked to the passenger side and collected what she needed. She tied the parka around her waist. It was too hot even at this hour to wear it for long. The bracelet she attached to her wrist keeping her elbow bent with her arm up afraid it'd slip right off. Then she picked up the paper with her son's picture and walked out of the lot toward where Rogers lived.

All of the lights were off at his house. She hoped maybe there would be the sound of a television when she approached the door. She knocked on the door to the porch first, not expecting it to be heard inside. The screen door wasn't closed all the way, and when she tried the door knob on the wooden door behind it, she found it was unlocked. Once the doors closed behind her on the porch, she couldn't see anything.

She opened the outside door behind her to let some light from the street shine in and went to the main door. The porch was covered in windows on all sides, and the blinds could be seen from the outside. Now she could see that black trash bags had been taped across them on the inside for added privacy. She rang the doorbell, but didn't hear it make a sound. She knocked, but there was no answer. She knocked again, harder this time. There was no movement in the house.

'Maybe he's not home,' she thought.

Eileen looked around the porch. It was filled with clutter. There were two sets of metal shelves normally found in a garage. They were filled with everything from garden fertilizer and old paint cans to toilet paper and canned goods. Off to one side there was a snowman and Santa blow mold, boxes of who knows what along the walls, and random other junk scattered all around. In the corner farthest from the doors, she spied a folded fishing chair leaning against the window.

She opened it and gently tested it before putting her full weight on it. Then she carefully positioned it behind Frosty without moving any items too much where it might easily be noticed that someone had been there. She closed the porch door and was surrounded by pitch darkness. She tried to carefully make her way to the chair to wait, but tripped several times in the maze as she went.

Sitting in the darkness, there was no concept of time passing. Her phone was in her SUV for a multitude of reasons. The main one being she didn't want to risk leaving anything behind at the crime scene. It rarely had more than a ten percent charge which meant it wouldn't have lasted long to alleviate her boredom. Not that it mattered. Even with a full charge, the last prepaid card she bought was almost out.

When she fled with her son, she would purchase a new phone after the plane landed safely in a new country, on a new continent where no one would know them. It would be a waste of what precious resources she had left to buy another card for this phone before then.

Lastly, she needed the element of surprise on her side. The sound of a phone ringing would give away her presence. If she set it on quiet, the vibration in her pocket from one of Remus's texts could startle her enough to give Rogers the upper hand.

Without it, without the ability to look at the screen to see the time, moments dragged on for hours, and hours could pass in minutes. All she knew was she sat there long enough she could've drifted into madness several times if she hadn't the strength left to fight it.

Eileen had grown accustomed to her surroundings. She leaned her head against the wall and closed her eyes to prevent her mind from trying to make out the shapes and shadows that lurked all around her. To keep the madness at bay, she played games in her head with her memories.

She remembered and relived all of Noah's birthday parties beginning with his first. His seventh birthday was her favorite of them. They had thrown Noah a surprise birthday party at the water park for him, and a dozen of his friends came.

Noah's last birthday was bittersweet. He invited two of his closest friends over for a campout in the backyard. They had ventured far enough on the property to hide their tents behind the trees. Her little man had been growing up, double digits. Unbeknownst to her son, she had stayed awake on the back porch all night in case any of them had needed her, but they never did. She spent the night reveling in admiration at him for being so strong and independent, taking pride in herself for raising such a capable young man, and also aching for the little boy who didn't like to stray far from his mama's side.

That's not why it was bittersweet. It was because it was the last of his birthdays she had been able to celebrate with him. The three that had passed since found her alone in the house with his favorite white cake and buttercream frosting, the cookie dough ice cream he loved so much, and the river of tears that flowed from her eyes.

She remembered his little league feats. The first time he was old enough to join up he had been so shy and nervous. Eileen had to run the bases with him. By the end of the season, he was out there on his own, taking to the game like he was born to play it. The first time he hit the ball without his tee stand she wanted to take him out for ice cream to celebrate. It was the first of only a handful of games his dad watched. Johnny hadn't seen the necessity to make a big deal out of it. "It was a hit, but it wasn't the game winning hit," he had said. Eileen dropped him at home and took Noah out to party without him. They had most of their fun without his father present.

There was his first homerun. She could hear the disappointment in his voice when he told her he didn't make pitcher and would play third base instead. Noah grew into that position and found joy and pride in playing it. He no longer needed his mom to hold his hand while he ran the bases, but every time he took the field, he would turn to the stands, find her face and smile. Part of the reason why she chose Montenegro is because there was baseball there for him.

Eileen was beginning to go through all of Noah's teachers starting with the private pre-school she had sent him to until Johnny put his foot down. His son wasn't going to grow up to be pampered. He insisted Noah attend public school instead.

That's when she heard the noise outside. She sat up and opened her eyes, listening carefully. It could just be someone walking by on the street, but the footsteps began drawing closer. When they made it to the front steps of Chuck Rogers' house, she leaned back and ducked her head hiding behind Frosty and Santa. If the door opened, enough light would shine in the porch where she could be detected if someone glanced her way. Her heart pounded in her chest, and she worried it was loud enough for him to hear.

She couldn't see him, but she could hear what he was doing. The outer screen door slammed shut loudly, but the porch door he left open, probably for light to see by. He mumbled and cursed, kicking junk out of his path as he walked. The sound of the keys clanging while he unlocked the main door to the house was loud, but not loud enough to make her feel like the sound of her thudding heartbeat couldn't be heard.

He opened the door and must have flipped a switch

because light from the house flooded the porch. Eileen ducked down ever lower, pulling her feet back under the chair until she almost collapsed it. She threw an arm out to the wall for balance and feared she was about to be discovered when all the light disappeared. He had closed the porch door and gone inside.

There was a lot of noise coming from the house. She could hear him mumbling and things being knocked around. There was a crash followed by a slur of curse words.

'He's drunk.' That would play into her favor. Driving a dagger into an elderly homeless man while he slept was easy compared to taking on Chuck Rogers. He was in his mid-forties, tall, and relatively fit. Being drunk gave her an advantage, but it also meant she didn't have much time to wait. Chances were he'd soon be passed out.

She hoped he would let her into his house, so she had to act while he was awake. If she had to break in, she risked injury and leaving more evidence behind.

The paper with Noah's picture on it was on the floor near her feet. She felt around until she found it. Then she made her way to the front door slowly using her feet as a blind cane to find any obstacles. Once there she held the missing flyer in her left hand and the bracelet in her right. She knocked on the door loudly then pressed on the eye to release the dagger, holding it at her side and toward her back to keep it out of view.

The door swung open, and Rogers towered over her. Light shone directly in her eyes and blinded her. "What do you want?" he growled.

The overwhelming stench of whiskey hit her senses, and she recoiled. Eileen lifted the flyer and asked, "Have you seen this boy?"

Rogers barely glanced at it before he said no.

"Please. Take a look. This is my son. He's missing."

"Sorry. Haven't seen him," he said and started to close the door.

She stuck her foot inside the frame preventing it from closing all the way and lifted her right arm to the door to press against it.

"What?" Rogers began before looking down at the bracelet and seeing the dagger that was exposed. "What are you doing?"

Eileen panicked. She thrust against the door with all her strength then drove the dagger into Rogers' chest, pulling it out quickly.

He stumbled backward and tried to swing at her. In his drunken state, it was easy for her to dodge his fist. The momentum continued to bring him around, and he fell flat on his face on the floor.

It was a tight fit because his body lay behind the door, but she squeezed in and threw herself on his back as he tried to stand. It was enough to knock him down again with her on top of him, bracing herself for the landing.

The dagger had come free and lay inches away from her. She grabbed it by the end of the bracelet and held it over him, straddling his back.

Rogers struggled beneath her. "Get off me!" he screamed. "You psycho!"

She waved the flyer in front of his face. "Look at him," she ordered. "This is my son. He died three years ago."

"I had nothing to do with it," he pleaded. "I don't even like boys."

'He thinks that's why I'm here, for revenge.'

"Just look at him. I'm going to bring him back to me," she explained, dropping the flyer by his face. "Your death will bring him back. I'm sorry," she said, driving the dagger into the back of his neck with both hands. She pulled it out and stabbed him again, and again.

Rogers had stopped moving. The blood that poured out of his wounds, down his neck was pooling up on the floor. It soaked the missing flyer she had created.

He appeared dead, but she wasn't sure. She lifted the bracelet one last time and thrust it into the right side of his skull. It was a move she soon regretted when it proved difficult to pull it out.

Once it was free, she snatched the blood soaked paper which tore effortlessly from the saturation. Eileen located all the bits and pieces she could, but it was hard finding the globs of paper in the thick puddle of blood.

She faced another challenge trying to stand up. There was very little room for her to move, but she managed to step back into the doorway. She stared at him for a long time looking for any sign of life, any sign that he was breathing or blinking of his eyes, anything that would tell her the job wasn't yet finished.

A car drove by outside, and she knew she needed to leave. It was unlikely that a person like Rogers would have many visitors, but it wasn't an impossible idea either. She took a couple steps back until she was on the porch and reached for the knob to shut the door, thinking better of it.

She lifted the parka over her head and lay the dagger and the bits of paper on it. She rolled the parka around it all to carry it back to the SUV. She walked across the porch and used a dangling sleeve to open the door trying to remember if she had used any precautions when she arrived to not leave fingerprints. She wiped the outer knob off with the sleeve just in case, but only succeeded in smearing blood on it.

That was when she ran. She bolted from the porch, down the walk, onto the sidewalk out front, then to the corner. She turned and ran the full length of that block before she rested. Her breathing was labored and erratic, and she knew she was about in the throes of hyperventilating. She bent over with the parka tucked under her right arm and put her left hand on her knee trying to take control with slow, deep breaths.

It was late, but there was plenty of light on the street. Her hand was covered in blood that glistened from the glow of the street lamp. When she removed it from her knee, she could see the imprints her bloody fingers had made. A wave of dizziness came on her, and she started to spin, almost falling over. She leaned against the stop sign and imagined sirens in the distance bearing down on her.

'*They aren't real,*' she told herself. '*But you need to get back.*'

She looked around to get herself orientated. She was two blocks from the far side of the parking lot. Her pace was fast, almost a slow trot. Every time she managed to slow to a normal pace her feet would instinctively speed up, trying to get her there as fast as they could.

Several of these houses were boarded up and emptied as the city bought them out, preparing to expand even further. Some still had people living in them, hanging on to their homes. There may even be squatters. Most of the people in this area would have their own reasons for not wanting to talk to the police, and she prayed that would be enough to save her because she had given anyone who had seen her a hundred reasons to be suspicious.

Eileen made it to her SUV. There were a lot of cars, but no people in the parking lot when she walked up. She opened the passenger door and reached for one of the plastic bags she had stored under the seat. The dome light showed her hands were covered in blood. She put the entire parka, bracelet and all, inside the bag. There'd be time to sort it out later.

The package of baby wipes were on the seat, and she pulled several out cleaning up as much of the blood, including what got on the handle when she opened the door as she could with them. She walked around and got into the driver's seat taking a look at herself in the mirror. A spray of blood hit her face when she first drove the blade into Rogers' neck causing her to flinch. She must have easily adapted and tuned it out after that because there was a lot more red streaks on her face then she had expected.

She whimpered pulling multiple wipes from the package and scrubbing at her face with enough pressure to take off a layer of skin along with his blood. There was no way she wouldn't be caught this time. Cries kept rising in her throat, but she swallowed them back. If she was going to have a mental break, it couldn't happen here. She needed to get to the cemetery.

It took dozens of wipes to scrub her face and the spots on her hands she had missed. She was finally happy with her reflection thinking she got it all wiped away.

When she started the car, the clock showed it was after two in the morning. She had been sitting on the porch for over three hours. It hadn't felt like that much time had passed.

She made her way to the cemetery not caring what route she took, not caring what security cameras might be able to identify her vehicle near the scene of a murder, not really caring about anything except her son. She pulled off the road and hid her SUV in the trees. That's when she allowed the panic to take hold and sobbed violently. The woods around here weren't the only witnesses to her outbursts, but she didn't care. The only people who could hear her were ghosts.

When she finally managed to pull herself together, she walked to the cemetery wall. She put her hands on the ledge to pull herself up, but a pain shot through her left wrist. There was enough light from the moon she could see it was swollen and starting to bruise.

It was a struggle, but she managed to pull her body onto the wall with one hand. She sat with her legs dangling over the edge. From where she rested she could see the mausoleum doors, and they were still shut. Her son hadn't left yet.

If the police came looking for her and didn't find her at home, this might be the next place they check. With her hand in the condition it was in, it would impede her escape. She decided to stay on the wall until her son emerged.

The pain that hadn't been noticed until she tried to put her weight on her wrist was increasing. A dull throb was constant with random sharp pains that shot up her arm. She tried, but couldn't remember how she had injured it.

Hours into her watch that night it hit her. When she jumped on Rogers' back and fell to the floor on top of him, she had put her hands out to brace herself. It had felt a little weird when they landed, but it hadn't bothered her again until she arrived at the cemetery.

Her hand had touched the tile floor. Her fingerprints would be there. She wondered if the police would dust that area. There were so many mistakes made this time. She couldn't remember opening the porch door, but she felt like she had used her hand instead of tucking it inside the parka. The chair she left in the corner of the porch where she waited probably collected loose strands of her hair. It was hard to know what other evidence she had left behind. Then, like an idiot, she had taken off in a sprint away from the house.

The dagger had to work this time. Eileen didn't believe she'd have the chance to try again before she was arrested. It had to work because she didn't have it in her to take another life.

'It's going to work,' she told herself. Tears dripped down her face. 'It has to. Any minute now, you're going to see movement on those doors because your son is trying to come out. Any minute now.'

Chapter Fourteen
That's Why

Eileen jerked awake, putting her hands down on the cemetery wall to catch herself from falling. Her left wrist cried out in pain. She had been desperate for sleep for quite a while and must've dozed off.

The dark night turned into a lighter shade of blue. It wouldn't be long until light started breaking over the horizon with the beautiful pink hues of the sunrise. There was still a little time left before she had to leave to avoid being detected, but she wasn't sure she could make it.

There was enough light to see the mausoleum doors were still closed. The chain was still threaded through the handles. It hadn't worked. For the second time in recent days, she would have to leave the cemetery without her son. She was a murderer twice over, and it had all been for nothing.

She climbed down the wall as carefully as possible, nursing her wrist. By the time she made it to her house, the pain in her wrist had grown to an unbearable throb, and her exhaustion was the worst it'd been since the early days after losing Noah. She pulled around the house and parked out back, too tired to deal with the locks on the front door.

The back door wasn't nearly as secure. The locks she purchased for the porch sat in the garage for months waiting on her to take the time to drill the holes. Then the power was shut off. She took them back to the store, pretending to have lost the receipt since their return policy had long expired for them. The key was hidden under one of the decorative rocks that trimmed her flower bed on the side of the porch. Once inside, she passed out on the kitchen floor just as dawn began to creep in through the patio doors.

When her eyes shot open, the first thought on her mind was the memory of the look on Rogers' face when she stabbed him. It was fleeting. All thoughts were quickly emptied from her mind by the intense pain in her wrist. Her bones creaked their complaints as she sat up using only her good hand for support. One look at her pained wrist told her she was not going to avoid seeing a doctor, and the sooner the better.

Eileen drug herself off the tiled floor and went to her SUV for the baby wipes. Lugging in the pans of water for a bath was out of the question. When she opened the passenger side door, she saw the bag with the bloody parka glaring back at her. *'Why not turn yourself in if you're going to leave evidence like this laying around?'* she belittled herself.

She grabbed the wipes and dug the bracelet out of the bag. She'd deal with the rest of it later.

The clothes she was wearing were carefully inspected when she took them off. There wasn't any blood that she noticed. She folded them and set them on the tank of the toilet. She used the wipes to wash her body, brushed some dry shampoo through her hair, and liberally apply deodorant. Digging through her tote, she pulled out the cleanest outfit she had to wear to the clinic. It could only generously be described as clean, but it would have to do.

Eileen was kicking herself for not taking better care of the dagger. As old as it was, it should have been wiped down when the blood was fresh. It was a miracle it was still in such amazing condition, but it wouldn't be for long if she didn't care for it properly. She pushed the eye to release the dagger and dried blood flaked off, falling on the edge of the sink and the floor.

She wiped the blade with a baby wipe, but it wouldn't come off easily. She wrapped a wipe around the padded end of the tongs she used for laundry and scratched at it until all of it picked off. Taking a new wipe, she cleaned the entire bracelet as much as she could. She wiped up the flakes of blood on the sink and what she could see on the floor. It wouldn't pass the inspection of a forensic team, but to the naked eye, it appeared fine.

On the way to the free clinic, she wondered what she should do with the parka. It was broad daylight, and she was nervous about someone seeing her throw something into a dumpster. People did it every day. She'd done it many times herself clearing up trash from her SUV. When you're tossing something you don't want anyone to find, it was a lot more nerve wracking than merely getting caught using the dumpster without authorization. It wasn't like any of the clerks were paid enough to care about who put what in their trash.

The parking lot of the clinic was almost empty, but that wasn't a trustworthy sign. Most of the people who came there arrived by bus or on foot. All of them would raise a judgmental eyebrow at the nice vehicle she drove, wondering how it was she couldn't afford to pay for health care. With that in mind, she passed the clinic and parked a block down the street.

She walked down the sidewalk carrying the tied off plastic bag containing the parka and the bloody wipes. A wide smile spread on her face. It was almost empowering, and she held her head a little higher than she normally would. There was evidence in her hand to convict her of murder, but no one was the wiser. A couple people walked on the street. A bum lay back on a bus stop bench as she walked past. Others drove by on the road. They were all now witnesses to something without realizing it.

Outside the clinic entrance, she shoved the bag into the trash bin.

Three hours later she left the clinic with a sturdy removable splint on her wrist and a prescription for pain killers. It was a clean, stable break, so she managed to convince the doctor a splint would work far better in her living conditions than a cast. She had to pay for it though at a discount. The clinic was free based on income, but that meant the services provided were cheaper than what you would receive at a regular doctor's office with insurance. The clinic probably still used the clunky old style plaster casts instead of the modern synthetic ones.

That wasn't the issue. She wanted to be able to remove it if necessary. A cast would raise eyebrows about how she injured herself. There were some questions she didn't want to have to answer. The prescription was a temporary supply. The clinic had made a follow up appointment for her at an orthopedic office and gave her the low income paperwork to take with her.

The appointment was in three days, but she had no intention of keeping it. She'd take one pill now in the hopes of having some relief from the never ending pain that pulsated in her wrist, but the rest she would save and use sparingly. With her son's body still in his coffin, her work wasn't done. She may need something to help with the pain when it was time to try again.

On the way to her house, she passed two boys on the

winding road outside the city. They were walking their bicycles through the grass a couple feet from the road around the curve the way she had taught her son. It doesn't matter what you teach your kids, or how much you try to keep them safe if the driver barreling down the road has had a little too much to drink when they get behind the wheel.

Eileen pulled up in front of her house without remembering the rest of the drive. She was lost in her head, wrapped up in her memories of Noah, and the night she let him down by not being there for him.

It was when she finally had enough of Johnny and his cheating ways. The affairs weren't so secret. Eileen *knew* what was going on. She wasn't oblivious, but she did turn a blind eye to it. There's a difference between knowing and having proof. And, that's what she was after that night: proof.

She used to want to believe there was a time when Johnny really did care for her. When they met in college, she wanted to believe he fell in love with her and wasn't only with her because her dad was rich. When he proposed, she wanted to believe it was because Johnny couldn't see himself spending the rest of his life with anyone else not because her dad had been diagnosed with cancer and didn't have long to live. She wanted to believe those things, so she chose to believe it early on when she first suspected there was someone else.

There was always somebody else. Johnny had a string of affairs. The earliest one Eileen figured out was when she was pregnant with their son, but there were probably others before that. Then Noah came along, and she loved him so much she didn't care.

The day she finally had enough, the final straw was shortly

after Johnny began seeing the woman who was now his second wife. Meredith was the new bookkeeper for his landscaping business. A business he began with her daddy's money. He would be nothing if it hadn't been for Eileen.

It was tired, tacky, and cliché, but that was his MO. He'd have an affair with the cute female in the office. When it ended, he'd find someone new, just as attractive and offer her a job.

Eileen decided to surprise him at work one day with lunch. She knew he'd be at the nursery. He had several landscaping crews and many company contracts, but the brick and mortar was a nursery with private retail sales and a small staff.

When she walked through the door, she could see through the office windows that Johnny was on the phone. Not wanting to cause an interruption, she waited nearby. While she waited, one of the shop employees asked if she needed anything.

"No, I'm good. I'm waiting for Johnny," Eileen said, holding up the bag she brought. "I thought I'd be romantic and surprise him with lunch."

"Oh, I'm sorry, Meredith," the girl replied. "I'm new. I haven't paired everyone's faces to their names yet." The girl smiled and walked away.

It wasn't the confirmation of the affair. She wasn't an idiot. She knew what was going on behind her back. It was the realization that everyone knew. That's what humiliated her. She'd never be able to show her face again around any of her friends. The constant wondering about how long they kept his secret from her would be too much.

Eileen left without a word to Johnny, without him ever realizing she had been there. She did her research and found where Meredith lived. The next time Johnny came up with some excuse why he couldn't be home she parked down the street from Meredith's and waited. It didn't take long for him to pull up and go inside for a few minutes before they left together.

Noah was staying the night at a friend's house, so she didn't have to worry about him. Eileen followed her husband to a restaurant where he and his mistress went inside. It was a restaurant he'd refused to take her to. "It was too hoity toity for his tastes," he had said.

Yet Meredith was good enough for him to go there. Eileen watched through the large open blinded windows as they were seated. Her jacket was still in the backseat from the last time it rained. It was hot and humid out, but she put it on and pulled up the hood to go inside. When the hostess seated her, she requested a table across the restaurant where she could keep an eye on Johnny in the hopes he would not take notice of her.

It was that night she knew he had never loved her. The way he looked at Meredith, the sparkle in his eye, the smile that came easily never forced. He had never looked at her like that. Eileen couldn't really say if what he felt for Meredith was love, but it was something more than he had ever felt for her.

While she watched, her phone rang, and it scared her to death. It was a friend of hers. She dismissed the call and looked around quickly, hoping it hadn't caught Johnny's attention. He was too lost in Meredith's beauty to care. Eileen put her on quiet mode and tucked it back in her person to prevent it from happening again.

That's why she didn't know Noah needed her. That's why she didn't answer when he called. Noah and his friend had got into a fight, and he wanted to come home. After trying his mom several times without an answer, he decided to ride on his bike alone. He knew the route well.

His friend's mom offered to drive him, but the friend would have to ride along with them. Noah refused the ride. Eileen always thought it was because he didn't want to sit in the car with his friend while they were mad at each other. Her son had lied and told the woman he was going outside to wait for his mom to pick him up.

Maybe it wasn't a full lie. Maybe that was why he went outside. He thought she would call him back soon like she always did, and be on her way. Eileen would've been there in a heartbeat if she knew her son needed her. Instead she sat in a restaurant, watching the jerk she had trusted her future to make a fool out of her oblivious to her son and his needs.

Whatever happened, whatever went through his mind that night, he ended up riding his bike toward home. It was too late and too dark for a ten year old to be riding his bike by himself, but that wasn't what caused the accident.

The Canyon Creek Bridge is well lit, but there was no pedestrian path on the side which made it dangerous for people crossing on foot or bicycle. Her son should have been, would have been seen if Billy Tucker hadn't driven home from a party after a few drinks. Of course he got a slap on the wrists. Her money in no way matched his fame. He was beloved by everyone. A local boy who made a name for himself until the career ending knee injury his first season. That didn't stop the endorsement contracts from coming in to increase his notoriety and bank account.

Not only had he been drinking, but he was in a hurry. His wife needed him. They both lost children that night. The difference was his hadn't been born while Eileen had ten years of memories to haunt her.

Eileen spent several days puttering around her empty home, talking to herself and the ghost that ran in and out. Twice she ventured outside to listen to the radio while charging her phone in the SUV. There had been nothing new from Remus. At least nothing exciting enough to warrant her contacting him. There was also nothing on the news about the death of Chuck Rogers.

She didn't imagine a monster like that would have too many people in his life. Any family and friends he may have had at one time would have turned their backs when he was accused. It was possible his body lay rotting just inside the front door of his home, and no one knew he was dead. Eventually he'd miss a meeting with his parole officer, and someone would come out to his house to check and discover him if the neighbors didn't notice a horrid odor first. She hoped she was long gone before that happened.

Chapter Fifteen

Moments

After a few days, her own body's stench was becoming a problem. Her wrist still ached far too bad for her to lug the pans in for a bath. It had been attempted, but even filling the pans only half full was too much for her to lift.

There was enough money left from the sale of her paintings, but she hadn't wanted to spend all of it before she was reunited with her son. It didn't look like there was much choice.

She removed the bracelet from her wrist that she had been wearing almost constantly. It called to her wanting to stay close on her arm. People might think she was crazy if she spoke those words out loud. It didn't matter. Maybe she was. The bracelet wanted to be on her arm just as much as she wanted to be close to it. It wasn't needed for what she was going to do. She didn't want to risk it getting lost or stolen.

Setting it on the kitchen counter, she went through her house gathering all of her clothes. The old shabby pieces she'd been wearing for years and the newer outfits she'd taken from the duffel bag were scattered everywhere. They lay on the floor wherever she tossed them when changing outfits. The hallway, kitchen and bathroom were the main rooms she limited herself to, and clothes, food packaging and assorted trash littered all of those rooms from her current stay. One shirt had a granola wrapper stuck to it that attracted an army of ants interested in the crumbs, but she barely noticed. The wrapper was tossed back on the floor after she peeled it off the sleeve.

Everything was brought to the SUV. It took several trips since she couldn't carry anything in her left hand. Her clothes were tossed in the tote except for the one outfit left from the duffel that was still clean. The tote, book bag and duffel were all piled into the backseat. She walked carefully behind the garage around where she parked making sure she didn't misstep. No water meant creating an alternative bathroom.

Once it was loaded, she started it up and backed it out, pulling up near the back of the house before stopping. Eileen darted into the house for one last thing. She grabbed the bracelet off the counter and slid it on her wrist. A sigh of relief came naturally, and she closed her eyes to revel in the comforting feeling of being home.

Eileen made her way to the truck stop connected to her favorite diner to pay for a shower. It was frivolous. Something she despised doing. After making the decision to allow her utilities to be shut off to save money, she would come to the truck stop often, as much as once a week. She still boiled water for baths back then or at the very least to wash up in between showers. As the months went by, she began to cut out the amount of times she paid for something she could manage herself at home.

The feel of the hot water cascading over skin was like heaven. It made her feel cleansed and relaxed. There was nothing like the spray from the shower head to make her feel human again.

Over time, her vanity became just as lost to her as her son. She would stand in the scalding spray until her skin mimicked a boiled lobster. Then she'd pamper her scorched body with products that were remnants of her former life. There were designer cosmetics, creams and lotions she already owned that would later become knock off versions until finally settling on whatever was on sale at the supercenter.

One day she dropped her mascara wand on the floor of the truck stop restroom. She stared at it mortified, not wanting to use it again, unsure of how much bacteria bred on the tile. She barely wanted to pick it up to toss it in the trash. There wasn't enough soap in the dispensers to scrub her hands clean afterward. When she looked in the mirror, the absurdity of her reflection began her wake up call.

The left eye was finished with the lashes pumped out. The other eye was bare. Without the mascara wand, she needed to figure something out and fast. Otherwise she'd walk out of there looking ridiculous. She began gently removing the mascara that had been applied. It was one of her two never leave home without, mandatory make up needs.

While she worked on taking it off, she thought of her son who would've been turning twelve soon. He'd never have to worry about a bad hair day or a pimple. He'd never know the anxiety of going out in public while feeling like he looked ridiculous. As she thought about him, she scrubbed at her face harder until her reflection looked more like a comical mug shot photo taken after a long night of drinking.

Instead of removing the mascara, she had smeared it across her face. Eileen put her hands on the edge of the sink and bowed her head, sobbing softly. It wasn't fair. It was wrong of her to continue to put her best look forward while her son's handsome face was locked away from the world. She was failing him.

Eileen turned the water on and wet some paper towels, ridding her face of ever trace of the make-up she had just painstakingly applied. On the way out of the restroom, she tossed her cosmetic bag into the trash. The few scattered items she still had at home she held onto, but she didn't use them anymore.

That day she made herself a vow. When her work was completed, when she finally brought her son back like he wanted her to do, then she could put more focus on herself and her image. Until that day, everything needed to be about him, and for him.

The voice over the speakers in the truck stop announcing her number was ready for the shower interrupted her thoughts. She approached her cashier for the key and towels then headed to the shower room. Once inside an uneasy feeling grew in her stomach. It sickened her to throw away another fifteen dollars on something like this, but she knew she should be grateful it wasn't coming out of the duffel bag yet.

She stripped down carefully removing her splint and stood under the shower head. The water was warm at first, and she slowly adjusted it until it was as hot as she could handle. The book bag was hanging on a hook nearby, and she pulled out the plastic bag containing the few toiletries she owned. With it, the bracelet came out and fell to the floor, clanging at her feet.

It startled her, and she jumped back almost slipping on the tile. She picked it up quickly, eyeing it for damage, but didn't see any. There was a strong pull drawing her to it, and she slipped it on her arm, holding her arms out from the spray trying to keep it dry. The eye asked her to reveal its secret, and she obliged.

Mesmerized, she brought her other hand to it and traced the blade, curving her finger over the pointed tip. As she did so, it pierced her skin. A tiny pain with a lot of blood followed.

In that instant, Eileen would've sworn she heard her son call out to her. "Mommy!" His voice sounded terrified, and there was nothing she could do to comfort him. It was all in her head. Everything had been in her head. That's the one thing she heard from everybody constantly since the accident. It wasn't a figment of her imagination though. It felt *real*.

Eileen raced through the rest of her shower, no longer caring if she got her fifteen dollars' worth or not. She dried off and took the outfit from the book bag. It was the last of the travel outfits she had stashed away in the duffel a long time ago, and it was the only clothing she owned that was clean.

As she brushed her hair, she wished she still had some kind of product, something to help shape it from the dingy, straw like structure that it normally possessed. There was a discarded stretchy hairband on the shelf under the mirror. Eileen glanced at it out of the corner of her eye several times before picking it up with a sigh. It would be obvious to anyone she was a couple steps past being worried about cooties.

She gathered her hair up behind her head and tied it off in a ponytail. As simple as the look was, it felt good to see a different version of herself staring back at her. All that was left was putting the bracelet back on her arm, and she was ready to leave.

Eileen handled the towels and returned the key. Skipping the salad bar in the truck stop restaurant she had planned on treating herself to, she headed straight to the laundromat.

At the Quick Wash, she brought in one of her near empty

detergent bottles that she had added a little water to from the pump at home. She emptied the contents of the tote bag into one machine and doused it with the soapy liquid from the detergent bottle.

Eileen stared into the drum and shook her head. It was someone else leading a different life, an alternate reality version of her who used to meticulously sort through the clothing by colors, material, and laundry care tag instructions. For every load, the dials on her washing machine would have been adjusted for temperature, fabric type and other cycle settings.

Some loads were pre-soaked. Some washed in hot. Others rinsed in cold. There had never been a full load of laundry done in her life, but she had come close. Most loads were barely a quarter full.

The dryer settings were just as diligent. They dried on high, on low. Some dried on a rack. Then she collected the inheritance from her father and hired a maid whose duties including the hassle of the laundry.

Eileen put the quarters in the slot, closed the lid, and pushed the button to start it. She let out a long breath not caring what the settings were any longer. It took months of wringing out the clothes in her bathtub before she realized her maid probably never cared either. If she was a betting woman, she'd put money on her maid tossing everything together, making her job simpler and freeing time to get her other work done.

The laundromat wasn't empty, but it wasn't busy. There were a couple tables open, but she noticed the row of chairs along the front windows had outlets at either end. She sat at the unoccupied end of the row and plugged in her phone. It wasn't dead because she had charged it on the way to the truck stop and again on the way here, but she turned it on now that she had time to kill.

The dings and chimes went off like firecrackers when she powered it on. It vibrated in her hand for several minutes as the notifications loaded. It raised eyebrows from the four other people in the building as her phone's concert didn't seem to end. She didn't mind. The lesson about leaving her phone on quiet had been learned loud and clear. It may not always have a charge. It may not always be turned on, but she would never silence it again.

They were all from Remus of course except for a couple random spam numbers. Ignoring the voice mails altogether, she opened the texting screen and looked at the last message he had sent. "Where are you?"

"At the laundromat," she replied.

"Give me the address," he sent.

"It's the Quick Wash on Beaumont. I don't know the number." She followed it quickly with another message. "Where are you?"

"At your house," he replied. "Scroll up. I'm on my way."

Eileen read through the rest of the messages. It was more of the same.

"News on the dagger..."

"Are you okay?"

"Been trying to get ahold of you..."

"Thought I'd take you out to dinner. Your spirits could use a lift."

So that's why he's here,' she thought, relieved she had taken a shower.

Depending on traffic and how well he knew where to go, it would take Remus about twenty minutes to reach the laundromat from her house. The clothes might be ready for the dryer before he arrived.

There were three television screens on the wall showing sports, old sitcom reruns, but the one nearest to her had a news channel on. She couldn't hear it very well over the laugh tracks from the sitcom. The captions were loading, and she read the words across the bottom of the screen.

The top story was about a young girl around twelve years old who had been found wandering in the woods. The police were having trouble identifying her, so the speculation was she must not be local.

Eileen unplugged her phone and moved to one of the empty tables closer to the television airing reruns. She wondered what kind of trauma the young girl had been through to cause her to forget her own name or be too afraid to speak it. The girl was alive, so it was the only reason Eileen could figure to cause the delay in identification. It warmed her heart this child would soon be reunited with her parents, but it broke her heart at the same time. Her son wasn't missing. She knew exactly where he was if only she knew precisely what she needed to do to bring him back.

It took a few minutes, but Eileen got caught up in the old barroom comedy. For the briefest of moments, there was nothing else. There were no thoughts of a dilapidated estate, of hunger pains from a stomach that hadn't been fed on a regular schedule for years, of a worn out reflection in the mirror, of a marriage failed, a son lost, and a life lived utterly alone. There was nothing, but the tired, dated jokes that wouldn't live up to today's television standards. For those few glorious moments, she had managed to escape her life.

Then Remus placed his hand on her shoulder while softly saying her name. Eileen jumped out of the chair and almost toppled it.

"I didn't mean to startle you," he said, hiding a chuckle.

She glared at him with her hand on her chest, trying to regain control of her heart rate. With her thoughts firmly planted back in reality, she checked the time. The clothes cycle would've ended several minutes ago. Giving Remus another scowl, she walked to the machine without a word and switched her clothes to the dryer.

Chapter Sixteen
Grounded

Noah knelt on the floor of Landon's bedroom holding an unfolded direction sheet probably half as tall as he was, trying to figure out how exactly the next section of the Lego castle was put together. The castle barely held his interest, but helping build it was slightly less boring than watching his friend do it. Although it was a lot more frustrating.

He and Landon had barely spoken for the last hour. After dinner, he was ready to rush up to his friend's bedroom to play the new video game his mom bought him that afternoon before dropping him off. If he had been at home, he'd have been halfway to conquering the game before he ate because his mom didn't put limits on his electronics time. His friend's mom did, but that wasn't why he was mad.

Landon was limited to an hour a day, but his mom made exceptions for things like sleepovers. They should've been able to spend the entire night exploring the levels, finishing quests, and moving closer to the big battle at the end. Instead, he was on the floor helping his friend with a Lego kit.

'Legos are so dumb. They're childish,' Noah thought. *'I stopped playing with these last summer.'*

His friend hadn't finished his chores during the week and lost electronic privileges for the entire weekend. His mom refused to budge and make an exception for Noah no matter how much they begged. They even offered to do a few chores to earn it, but nothing worked. In fact, she threatened to take

Noah home if they kept it up. That ended their please immediately. Neither of them could've realized it would've been the best thing that could've happened that night.

Nothing had been said about not being able to play video games until Landon's mom mentioned it during dinner. *It's because he knew I wouldn't come,'* Noah fumed. That's what upset Noah the most. He'd been looking forward to playing his new game tonight. If he had known they couldn't, he would've gone ahead and tried it out that afternoon before coming over. He tried to convince himself he would've still come out for the sleepover, but the truth was he wasn't so sure.

Any other day he would've helped his friend build the castle. He'd tease Landon about being a baby playing with baby toys, but he'd build it. Landon knew he was getting the game today and how much he was looking forward to playing it. Noah believed he kept his grounding a secret on purpose.

Their plan was to stay up late and wait for Landon's parents to go to bed. They'd have to be quiet so they wouldn't get caught, but they'd finally be able to play it. The waiting was the hardest part. He didn't think it'd ever be time to sneak playing it. Not being loud during it was another battle. Noah had a tendency to yell at the characters on the screen even if they couldn't hear him. It'd be easy to slip up if he got excited.

Noah wasn't too worried about it. She couldn't punish him too much. The worst she could do was take him home where he'd be able to play his game anyway. She couldn't take the game away since it was Noah's. His friend was the one who'd suffer the consequences.

He sat on the floor fishing through hundreds of Legos trying to find the piece he needed. Out of the corner of his eye, he saw his new video game sitting next to the television. It was all he could think about it.

"I heard Mia likes you," Landon said unexpectedly.

Noah gripped his stomach with one hand and shoved the index finger of his other hand in his mouth pretending to gag.

Landon laughed. "Noah and Mia," he sang out sweetly, making kissy noises.

"Enough!" Noah yelled at him.

"I'm just joking around," his friend said. "But she does like you."

He shot Landon a glare, but didn't say anything. Noah knew he was teasing. He glanced again at the video game before returning his focus to the Legos. It's just that he was already mad.

"Well…" Noah had been waiting for the right moment to say this. "I heard you held Hailey's hand on the school bus yesterday."

Silence. Landon didn't acknowledge him.

Noah stopped searching through the Legos and looked at Landon. He was bent over so close to the floor Noah could barely see any of his face behind the partial castle they had built. But it looked like he was blushing. "You did not!"

He couldn't believe it. He assumed it was a rumor started by Hailey's friends meant to humiliate Landon. That's why he brought it up, to embarrass Landon like he'd just done to Noah. "You and Hailey?"

"She's nice," Landon said softly.

Noah fell back onto the floor as if he'd been shot, pretending to be dead.

"Stop," Landon was annoyed. "Don't act like you've never

thought about asking a girl out before because I know you have."

'No, he doesn't,' Noah thought. He'd never told his friend anything like that, but it was true. There was a girl he wanted to be friends with, but he wasn't going to hold her hand.

"Who is it?" Landon asked. "What girl do you like?"

"Em-" Noah began to answer, but stopped himself. He wasn't sure why he'd admit anything like this to anyone.

"Emily?" Landon sat up straight. His eyes widened, and his mouth dropped in shock. "You like Emily?"

"No! Gross. Not like that," Noah told him. "But I wouldn't mind playing video games with her."

Emily was the only kid at school who had been in his classroom every year. All the students were mixed up and thrown into different rooms with new faces each year. He and Emily had always had the same teacher. That's the only reason he learned so much about her. She was the only girl he knew who liked to play video games. If he was going to be friends with a girl, it was definitely her.

"She doesn't like you," Landon said.

The words hurt Noah in a way he didn't understand. He sat up and stared at Landon who was still rifling through Legos. "Why do you say that?"

Landon shrugged, "Because she doesn't."

"How do you know?" Noah found himself worrying it was something Emily had actually said to his friend.

"All you do is talk about baseball."

"Why were you talking to her about me?" Noah asked.

"I wasn't, but Hailey said you talk about baseball too much. Girls aren't into baseball, Noah. If you're not talking about video games, then you're talking about your team. I'm sure Emily thinks that too."

Noah became angrier. He stared at the half built castle, huffing air out from his mouth and nose. He wanted to hit it, to knock it across the room, breaking it into as many little pieces as he could. He would've done it too except he had been working so hard on it and was curious to see what it looked like when it was finished.

"Don't get mad at me," Landon said. "You're the one who won't shut up about playing third base."

"That's it!" Noah screamed as he jumped to his feet. "You're the one who didn't tell me you were grounded from electronics, and we couldn't play video games all weekend."

"What?" Landon was confused how they went from talking about Emily to him being the one who had done something wrong.

"Yeah. You should've told me we couldn't play video games. You knew I was bringing this new one today."

"No, I didn't," Landon said.

"Yeah huh," Noah insisted. "I've been talking about it all week."

"You said your mom would buy it for you on Friday. You never said you were planning on bringing it with you."

"Well, of course I would. You know that. We always play video games together."

"Is that the only reason why you come out here?" Landon asked.

Noah stopped himself from answering yes. Something told him it was wrong to say, but it was what they always did. His eyes darted to the game again. He supposed it wasn't the only reason he came out there, but he couldn't think of any others.

"It is!" Landon cried out. He grabbed the video game. "You care more about this stupid game you just got today then you do about me, and I'm your friend."

"I do not," Noah said, reaching for the game.

Landon lifted it over his head, out of Noah's reach. "Yeah you do."

"No, I don't," he said, trying to get it from him. Landon stood a couple inches taller than him which meant he could hold it just high enough to prevent Noah from getting it. "Stop. Give it to me."

"Just admit it," Landon said.

"No," Noah practically yelled.

The bedroom door opened, and Landon's mom appeared in the doorway. "What's going on in here?"

"Nothing," Landon said, handing the video game back to Noah.

Landon's mom spied the game in Noah's hand and crossed her arms. "You know you've lost electronics this weekend, Landon."

"We were just looking at the cover is all," Landon lied to her.

His friend's mom turned to Noah, and he nodded. It made him sick to cover for Landon. He didn't want him to get in trouble, but he was still pretty mad. It gave him an idea.

"I don't feel well," Noah said. He clutched his mid-section for emphasis.

"Oh? What's the matter?"

Noah moaned and said, "It's just my stomach." He felt fine, but he didn't want to be there anymore. "I think I'm going to call my mom," he said.

"Okay, sweetie," she said, putting her arm around his shoulders. "Come with me. Let me take your temperature."

Noah picked his cell phone off the floor and went with her into the bathroom still clutching the video game tightly. His temperature was normal, but he insisted his stomach was upset and said he wanted to go home. She told him she'd let Landon know he was leaving.

He called his mom to come pick him up, but there was no answer. Then he sent her a text message asking her to call him. He didn't give her a full minute to respond before he sent another one saying it was important. He wanted to go home.

When he went down the hall to Landon's room, he could hear him talking to his mom downstairs. "Honestly, mom, I don't know what's wrong. He didn't say anything until you came into the room."

"It didn't look that way to me," she scolded him. "It looked like I interrupted a fight that was about to break out."

"We were just goofing around. I told you." It sounded like Landon was on the verge of crying.

Noah rolled his eyes. His friend was trying to get out of being in any more trouble than he already was. He thought about going down there and telling his mom the truth, but he would never do that. The thought made him smile though. It felt good knowing he held Landon's fate in his hands. It wouldn't take much, and his friend's mom would be furious, loading them both in the van to take Noah home. He sighed and walked away toward his friend's room. This wasn't their first fight. They'd be fine by the end of the weekend.

In Landon's room, he grabbed his overnight bag and

looked around to make sure he wasn't forgetting anything else before heading to the stairs. He glance at the Lego structure on the floor. Part of him wanted to finish building it. Part of him still wanted to knock it across Landon's room.

He walked downstairs with his bag in his hand. "Is your mom on her way to pick you up? Or do I need to give you a ride home?"

For a minute, he thought about taking the ride. The quicker he left the better. Landon would have to be in the van with him because his dad wasn't home to watch him. He didn't want to spend another minute with him tonight.

"No, she's going to come get me." It was becoming easier to lie to her. "I'm going to wait on the porch for her if that's okay. I think the fresh air might help me feel better."

Landon's mom tilted her head to the side in thought and smiled. "Sure thing, Noah. Go on ahead. Just let me know when you leave, okay?"

"I'll go wait with him," Landon volunteered.

It almost made Noah throw up which would've made his story about the fake belly ache more believable. He was going home to get away from Landon. The last thing he wanted was to be stuck with him until his mom showed up.

"No, you stay in here," Landon's mom said. "The last thing I need is you getting sick too. Hopefully, you haven't already caught whatever it is he has."

Noah walked outside. He checked his phone, but his mom still hadn't responded. *Maybe she's already on her way,* he thought. He called her again, and it went to voice mail. This time he left a message. "Mom, where are you? I need you to come get me. Landon and I got in a fight. I want to go home."

He waited about ten minutes. That's what his phone said from the calls and texts he was sending. It felt more like an hour. If his mom was already on her way, she'd be there any minute. Landon's mom would come check on him soon, and he was shocked she hadn't already. He didn't want her coming out and asking more questions. It'd only end with her driving him home once she found out he couldn't get ahold of his mom. She'd probably fallen asleep early which meant she was at the house. He could go home.

Not wanting to risk being stuck at Landon's, he tried his mom one last time, but he got her voice mail again. "Hey. I'm just going to ride my bike home. I don't want to be stuck in the van with Landon while his mom drives me. I just don't want to be around him right now. I'll be fine. I know the way, and I know how to be safe. I'll see you soon, mom. I love you. Bye."

Noah straddled his bike and slung the long strap of his duffle bag across his chest diagonally, hanging it over his back. The weight of it threw off his balance on his bike a little bit, but he didn't think it'd be much of a problem. He pushed off and started riding his bike down the driveway and turned at the end of it, staying close to the side of the road. His face was red hot, and he felt a flurry of nervous excitement in his stomach. He was afraid someone was watching him leave and would soon be outside yelling his name to stop him.

A couple blocks away he tried to look back over his shoulder to see if he recognized any of the vehicles heading his way. Each time he tried the off centered weight of the bag on his back would cause him to lose his balance, and he'd almost wreck. He didn't feel safe until he made it to the road just outside the city which led to his house. It was only a five minute drive from his house to Landon's. Noah didn't know how long it would take by bike, but he was in the home stretch now. It wouldn't be long before he was home.

He stuck to the edge of the road like his mom had taught him. There were no sidewalks to ride down. It was dark in parts, so he used the flashlight from his phone to help him see.

When the Canyon Creek Bridge loomed in the distance, he began to regret leaving Landon's so hastily. He never had liked this bridge. There was no shoulder, no gravel off the pavement, and certainly no walkway built along the side. The bridge had always seemed too small to him. Whenever his mom drove across it while passing another car, he'd squeeze his eyes shut tightly. It didn't seem like there'd be enough room for two cars at once, side by side, but they never wrecked.

About halfway across the bridge, he heard the car approaching before he saw the headlights. The screeching tires and the rumbling of the engine were loud. Then the headlights drew closer from behind, illuminating the bridge more clearly. He was thankful there wasn't another car coming from the opposite direction because there definitely wasn't enough room for two cars and a bicycle.

As the car came closer, it made him nervous. He was flooded with light now. It made it seem like it wasn't just a car, but some gargantuan vehicle which could take up the full width of the road, both lanes. He knew it was close. It was right behind him, and he hoped there was enough room.

Noah turned his head back to check, and the weight of his duffle bag shifted. He lost his balance, but this time he couldn't correct it. His bike went down right in front of the car.

He felt the impact no worse than falling off his bed to the

floor which didn't seem right to him. Then his body flew into the air with the bicycle. Everything moved in slow motion, and it was almost like he was watching it happen instead of suffering it himself. One leg went through the frame, and when his body fell back onto the pavement, the bike grotesquely twisted his leg to the side. Noah didn't notice. He felt his body hit the road. There was a sharp sting in the back of his head. Then there was nothing.

A funny thought popped in his head as soon as he landed. *'Now, we're both grounded.'* It had to be a good thing he could still make jokes he thought.

It surprised him how little he hurt. There was darkness all around, and he tried to open his eyes. He felt like he couldn't get them to work then he realized they were open. He just couldn't see. Before he could panic thinking he'd been blinded, he felt weightless like he was floating on water. It was the last thing he would ever experience.

Chapter Seventeen
Hard to Stay Hidden

Eileen stood in front of the dryer, clutching her book bag which doubled as a purse tightly. She always ritualistically watched the cycle begin and made sure it was running fine as if not doing so would certainly ensure there would be a problem. Some hiccup in the operation of the machine which would delay her time at the laundromat.

She had lost herself for a moment in the television show she had been watching. That hadn't happened in as long as she could remember. It felt almost nice to be normal again even if briefly, but it also made her feel guilty.

If the aftermath of Remus startling her, she appreciated how lucky she was. It had been a close call. After he told her that he was on his way, she had toyed with the bracelet, understanding it needed to be hidden before he arrived. It wasn't worth the risk of him trying to take it back. She was too weak to fight for it and win.

It didn't want to leave her arm. It begged her to remain. It cried out when she pried it off and placed it in the outside pocket of her book bag in the hopes Remus wouldn't realize how close he was to it. She didn't need to take the book bag with her when she switched out the clothes. All she needed was the six quarters necessary to start the dry cycle, but she couldn't leave it behind next to him. It was too risky.

'What if he noticed the odd shaped bump in the front pocket?' she thought. *'It wouldn't take much for him to figure out it was*

the dagger.'

Eileen glanced across the room at him, but his focus was on the next sitcom being aired. Part of her wished she had left the dagger at home. She wouldn't be feeling this disconcerting unease, but another part was thankful it was close by. Remus had gone to her house looking for her. *'What if he had gone inside?'* The front door might be padlocked, but he knew how to slip in the back.

'Doesn't he?' she thought. Eileen scrambled to think of the last time he had been at her house, of all the times he had been there. Her mind was drawing a blank. The only thing clear in her head was the dagger and keeping it safe. It was like her brain refused to be concerned with anything else.

When her feet finally made their way back to the hard plastic empty chair next to Remus and sat down, he smiled at her. "How are you doing?" he asked.

'He knows. He knows everything.'

"Same as always," she sighed. "Hanging in there."

"What happened to your arm?" He eyed the splint curiously.

She lied and said she slipped and fell. "I can be a klutz at times," she told him. "I put my hand out to block the fall and broke my wrist."

"How'd you fall?" His eyes hadn't left her wrist once since asking about her injury.

It was obvious he didn't believe her. She wondered if he was trying to gauge if the bracelet could fit inside the splint unnoticed. The thought caused a flurry of excitement in her gut. It might work, but that wrist was useless for anything more than wearing it.

Without having an explanation for it in queue, she painted an impromptu picture with words on the spot. The official story now was that she sloshed some water out of the bucket she was carrying in from the well for a bath and slipped in it.

Remus nodded, but she caught a glimpse of something in his eyes. There was some thought or shadow of an idea that passed through his mind quickly. It must be the bracelet he was thinking about. He wants to get to the real reason behind his visit.

'He doesn't know how to bring it up,' she thought, *'but that's why he's here: to tell me he knows what I've done and take the dagger back.'*

"How long do you think?" he asked, nodding toward the row of machines.

Eileen shrugged, "Thirty-six minutes from when I started them. Depends on if they need longer than that to finish."

It was a lie of sorts. It would take a lot longer than that to dry the load, but those were the last six quarters she had. What wasn't dry in that time would hang over the rail of her back porch to finish drying in the fresh air.

"I'll take you anywhere you want to eat," he said.

She had forgotten he offered to take her to dinner.

"Name the place," he continued. "If they're busy, I'll give them a call to make a reservation."

"Road Plaza," she said.

Remus' eyes narrowed, and he stared at her in disbelief. "You could pick any place, and that's where you want to go?"

"Yeah." She shifted in her chair nervously. They had grown close, but their friendship had been based on a customer and salesman relationship. There hadn't been enough social visits for her to become accustomed to him outside the store. She managed to always wind up feeling judged which was nothing new. Everyone looked down their nose at her. Remus wasn't everyone though. His opinion still mattered to her.

"No, it's fine," Remus said. "I just thought... I don't know what I thought. I guess I assumed you'd pick someplace fancier."

"I don't need fancy," she said. Her words came out more tempered than she had intended. She took a deep breath and explained, "It's a good place. I feel comfortable there."

Remus nodded. "Road Plaza it is."

They didn't say much while waiting on the dryer. There wasn't much they could talk about in a place like this. Too many people were within earshot who might raise eyebrows over their topics of conversation. They passed the time watching television. Remus was more caught up in the next sitcom episode than Eileen. She kept the book bag between her feet on the floor with her shins squeezing it between her legs. As long as she could feel the bracelet, everything was fine.

The power of the dagger assaulted her from every direction. It wanted to be freed. It didn't appreciate its confinement. The bracelet was meant to be worn. It was a beautifully made trinket containing a deadly surprise. It wanted to be on her arm, and it begged her to release its inner secret, astonishing others with its mystery. She couldn't see to its demands around Remus. It had to be kept stashed away. While he hadn't made mention of it directly, it was drowning his thoughts as well. The bracelet was what he was really after regardless of the pretense he laid out for his visit.

It was an agonizing wait for the dryer. The spinning of the

drum finally slowed and then ceased altogether. Eileen jumped to her feet, grabbing all three of her bags and carrying them to the dryer. All of the clothes were still damp more so than she anticipated. She wished she had a few more quarters, but she didn't dream of asking Remus for anything else.

Eileen thought about going home right away to hang them before they had a chance to wrinkle too badly. Trying to keep wrinkles out of her clothing was one of the few vanities she could still cling to because it cost nothing. She kept seeing Remus find the bracelet in her book bag while she hung the clothes over the rail. If he noticed how reluctant she was to part with the book bag, even for the smallest moment, he'd eventually figure out what she was hiding in it.

She folded everything carefully and tried to fit as much as she could inside the two larger bags without having to use the book bag for any of it. When she picked everything up to walk toward Remus, he met her across the room, taking the bags of clothing from her which she allowed him to do. Her hand remained clamped tight on the book bag.

"It's up to you," he said. "Do you want to drop the clothes at your house first? Before we eat?"

Eileen held the door to the laundromat open for him. He walked outside and looked around for her car. She nodded up the hill, and he followed her.

"It's no problem," he continued, walking toward her SUV.

The thought was appealing, and she almost answered yes impulsively. The bracelet whispered to her again, reminding her that he might grow suspicious of her unwillingness to put the book bag down while taking care of her laundry. "No," she said instead. Wrinkled clothing wasn't the furthest fall from grace she'd experienced. "It's fine."

"Do you want to take my vehicle?"

Eileen froze in place causing Remus to bump into her back on the sidewalk. *'My car?'* she thought. She needed to get gas, but had forgotten.

There was enough for the car to make it to the house, but not enough to make it home and back to the gas station later after grabbing something else to sell. She hadn't planned on drying her clothes at all. Those quarters were earmarked for the gas tank. The unexpected visit threw her off, and she forgot her original plan. All that was left was the remaining $1.24 in assorted small change. She'd have to put that in her tank before she did anything else.

"What?" he asked. "We don't have to take my truck. Besides, I was going to fill your tank while I was here anyway."

"You don't have to do that," she said quietly. It bothered her when people offered her handouts. It was happening more often the worse her living situation became.

"Who said anything about have to?" he asked, setting her bags in the back of her car. "I want to."

Eileen climbed into the driver's seat and buckled her seat belt. She put her book bag between her body and the door, keeping the dagger as close to her, and as far from Remus, as she could manage. If he thought it strange for her to do that instead of tossing it into the back seat, he kept that opinion to himself. He didn't have to voice it because she was positive he was suspicious of her every move by now.

At the truck stop, she pulled up to a free pump and sat in the car while Remus got out. He swiped his card and began to pump the gas. She watched with growing embarrassment as the dollar amount on the screen climbed higher and higher. She wondered if Remus was fully aware of what he was getting into when he offered to do this.

When he was done, she pulled around to the side and parked near the outside restaurant door. She walked inside with the book bag slung over one shoulder. The bracelet was screaming at her because it had been over an hour since it last touched her skin. It wanted her to leave him, to run when he wasn't looking. It had been kept locked away for far too long, and it demanded she give it the freedom it had been denied.

The waitress who approached to seat them had worked there for as long as Eileen had been a somewhat regular customer. She was a pleasant older woman with an old fashioned hairstyle. Eileen pictured the swirls of hair bobby pinned in place at night while the woman wrapped her head before laying down. The woman smiled at Eileen and cast a quick side eye in Remus' direction with a glint in her eye.

'It's not like that.' But, she understood why it might be assumed.

Glancing over her shoulder, the waitress said, "You're in luck. Your booth is open."

Eileen nodded at her awkwardly unsure of what to say.

The woman led them to her booth and placed a menu in front of Remus before hesitantly asking Eileen if she needed one. There were only two things she ever ordered here. It was always the breakfast special or just coffee while she charged her phone.

"Yeah," she said, sliding into the booth. "I think... I think I might."

She set the menu on the table. "Coffee?"

"With a tall glass of ice," Eileen added.

After asking Remus what he wanted to drink, the waitress left the table.

Eileen removed her phone and charger from her book bag and plugged it into the outlet under the table and slid the book bag under her leg until she could feel the bulging material which kept the bracelet from view. It melted layers of stress off her being able to feel it, to experience the security of it being with her. She hoped it was enough to satisfy the bracelet into leaving her alone until she was by herself at home.

She looked over the menu trying to decide what might keep best as leftovers. Her stomach growled in delight at every food option her eyes read. She wouldn't be able to eat a full meal. Her body wouldn't know what to do with that much food at once. It'd make her sick. By the time the waitress returned with their drinks, she still hadn't made up her mind. It had been far too long since she needed a menu here. She couldn't remember the last time she ordered anything other than the early bird special.

Remus excused himself to use the restroom while she continued to make up her mind. Once he was gone, she unzipped her book bag and removed one of several empty store bags she kept inside. She used her spoon to put one ice cube into her coffee to help it cool. The rest of the glass she dumped into the plastic bag and shoved it into her book bag. She placed the empty glass on the edge of the table to be picked up. After adjusting the book bag to feel the bracelet against her leg again, she went back to the menu until she made up her mind.

The glass was still on the side of the table when Remus returned, but if it raised any questions, he didn't say anything.

He had to wonder where it had gone. It was unlikely she ate sixteen ounces of ice in such a short period of time.

Their waitress made no mention of it either when she came back with her order pad in hand, but she had probably grown accustomed to Eileen's quirks and wasn't surprised by anything she did anymore. When it was her turn after Remus, she placed her order. "I'll have the BLT Club with fries."

"Soup or salad?"

"A salad with ranch on the side, but can I have it in a to-go box?" she asked.

"Sure thing." The waitress scribbled it on her pad. "Will that be all?"

Eileen nodded and watched the waitress' hand grab the empty glass as she walked away. She felt relieved to have it gone like it was evidence of her sad state, and she didn't want anyone else to see it. At the same time, she wondered if anyone would say anything if she had asked for a refill of ice.

"I could buy you something to take home if you need it," Remus said.

"No." Eileen shook her head.

"I mean it," he said. "It's no trouble."

Her cheeks flushed hot, and she imagined what shade of red they had darkened into. There he went with the charity again. "It's not that," she insisted. "I won't be able to eat it all, and I don't like for things to go to waste." Something in her tone told Remus to drop the subject.

They sat idly for a few minutes waiting for the tension to dissipate. The truck stop restaurant was littered with televisions. Each station playing had two screens broadcasting it around the room. The idea was that a customer could find something interesting to watch no matter where they sat. Two had a game on and two played music videos. One of the two televisions set to a local news station wasn't far behind Eileen. It was perfect for Remus to follow, but not her. Its twin was far across the restaurant. She could barely see it much less make out the scrolling captions at the bottom of the screen.

Eileen studied the other customers instead. She liked to imagine what it must be like to live a normal life. It had been so long she wasn't sure how lives were supposed to function anymore. Most of them were older men who had probably stopped to fuel and shower. There were always a few couples in the early morning. Tonight, there were a couple of families, and she was taken aback to see the children. *'Noah.'*

"How are you doing?" he asked.

She nodded and opened her mouth to answer.

"No. How are you *really*?"

It was a dumb question. She blinked back her tears. How was she supposed to be doing? She had lost everything in this life. The marriage to a man she once loved and would've done anything for had only been one sided. She lost her money, her fortune. She was destitute, barely a step above homeless. She even lost her name when she married the man who only said I do to her father's estate. Then she lost her son which was the most unbearable heartache anyone could experience. It was a heartache which never lessened, never went away. It's still with her every morning when she opens her eyes and has to face the reality that he's gone once again. It rips her heart out anew. She was on the verge of losing her sanity too if Noah wasn't reunited with her soon.

"Hey... Hey." Remus was saying softly. He reached across

the table with his hand. "I know it's hard. We're almost there, right?"

She didn't know how long he'd been trying to get her attention. She nodded weakly at him. The closer she got the harder it was to continue.

"Don't give up," he said.

Something on the screen behind her caught his attention, and he stared at it. Eileen looked across the room trying to follow it on the other television. It was more about the young girl who had been found wandering out of the woods. It looked like a press conference was being held outside someone's home. A couple – her parents probably – were trying to cover her face to shield her from the barrage of flashes going off all around them from photographers as they walked her inside.

"That poor girl," Remus muttered.

Eileen had heard something about it on the radio. She'd been hearing a lot about it actually whenever she was in her car. Authorities were tight lipped as to what they believed happened to her.

"Have you heard about this?" he asked. Before she could answer, he went on, "She was missing for two years then someone saw her wandering out of the woods near Hanover Park."

Remus went on talking about what was said on the news, but Eileen didn't hear him. There wasn't much to say anyway. The girl didn't remember anything since shortly after being taken. It was some sort of trauma induced amnesia.

The first time she heard those words on the radio she wondered what had to happen for it to take effect. Not remembering seemed like a blessing she'd have welcomed after losing Noah.

"They don't know who took her. Or they're not saying," he added.

It was for the best the girl couldn't remember, if she actually didn't remember anything. The horrors she'd endured the last two years would be difficult for anyone to work through, let alone someone so young. She was barely older than a baby.

"I won't ask you again." Remus' voice brought her back to her now cooled cup of coffee.

"What?" She lifted her mug and drank almost all of it.

"There's been a bunch of real life unexplained mysteries popping up lately haven't there?"

She shrugged her shoulders.

"It must be difficult to watch another family experience the reunion you've been desperately searching for." Remus shook his head. He propped his elbows on the table and rubbed his hands together before clasping his fingers and pressing his forehead against his folded hands. "Eileen, I've known you for a long time now, but I won't pretend to know what you're going through, what you've already suffered through."

The waitress arrived with their food checking to make sure everything was okay, and they didn't need anything else. "I'll be back with the coffee pot, hon, and you just let me know when you're ready for that salad."

Eileen gave a quick nod and began rearranging her food. She salted the fries and poured some ketchup on the side of the plate to dip them. The BLT Club would still be better than most of the meals she'd had recently in the morning, but the fries? Those needed to be devoured tonight if she wanted to enjoy them. After she swallowed the first one, her stomach screamed in appreciation and demanded the rest of them be shoveled down at once. She knew it would make her sick, so she ignored her gut, eating them slowly, one at a time.

Remus cut into his steak. The myoglobin leaked onto the plate making it look like it was still bleeding. It reminded her of the blood pouring out of the back of Chuck Rogers' neck while she stabbed him repeatedly, and her hand flew up to stop Remus from eating it. She caught herself in time and luckily he was too intent on cutting his steak to notice her.

She'd never thought she'd be capable of taking someone's life, let alone two grown men. Yet she'd done so easily. No, that was the wrong word. It wasn't easy, especially with Rogers who put up more of a fight. But there was no hesitation. She didn't stop and second guess herself. If she had, Rogers would've easily overtaken her and killed her instead.

By the seventh or eighth fry, she was already feeling full, but she pushed through. She managed to get about half of them down. If she ate anymore, she'd throw up. When the waitress checked on them, she asked for two small containers to put her sandwich and fries in separately.

She looked at the television again. The anchor was now discussing the gentlemen from Vietnam. She didn't know what was being sad, but there probably wasn't anything new. The government had been tight lipped regarding any new information about him. He'd face some serious charges before it was all said and done.

Eileen had ate too much. She was starting to feel sick and exhausted. All she wanted was to go home and rest her head.

His voice was cutting in and out as he talked to her about

the shop, about some products, about a few regular customers she'd seen there several times. It was hard for her to pay attention to most of what he was saying. Her thoughts kept being drawn back to the earlier news coverage of the mother being reunited with her little girl. The image of the mother smiling through her tears was seared into her brain. Someday, hopefully soon, that would be her.

"Is that going to stay fresh?" She heard Remus ask.

The waitress had dropped off the boxes and topped off her coffee without Eileen realizing she'd made another trip to the table. Eileen nodded as she put her sandwich in one and the rest of her fries in the other.

"Are you sure? There's mayo on that isn't there?"

She opened her book bag and took out her bag of ice carefully placing the containers inside of it. She wasn't sure if Remus was impressed or mortified, but he kept his opinions to himself.

"Well, let's get on with what you've been waiting for," he said.

Eileen leaned forward eager to hear exactly what she must do.

"I'm still waiting to hear back from my friend, the expert, to double check my translation."

Her shoulders slumped forward. This was taking too long. It should've been over by now. Get the dagger. Make a sacrifice. Save her son.

Remus looked around to make sure no one was in earshot. "But I believe this is going to be much more difficult than we had anticipated."

"How's that?" She was void of all emotion. Difficult didn't

come close to describing what she had been through. If this was merely going to be difficult, she could handle it.

"I think the sacrifice has to be the person responsible for the death of the one being resurrected."

Eileen tilted her head and raised an eyebrow. *'Billy Tucker.'*

"An eye for an eye, right?" Remus said. "You know who that means. It won't be easy."

She placed the palms of her hands on the edge of the table and pushed until her arms straightened and her back was touching the back of the booth. "It means I better be ready to run because I won't have long until the cops find me."

Remus studied her trying to gauge the head space she was in right now. "I'll give it another day or two," he said. "If I don't hear back from him by then, I'll check in and see if there's been any headway."

'Hopefully, it doesn't take too long,' she thought. *'Billy Tucker doesn't have a couple days left.'*

Chapter Eighteen
Party Time

Eileen had almost been wrong about how much time Tucker had left, almost as wrong as Remus had been about how soon his friend would get back to him with the translation. It wasn't going to be easy to get to him unnoticed.

She pulled into the parking lot of the Burger Shack with the windows rolled down. The voices of those in the drive thru carried into her car, and she listened as they ordered whatever they wanted to eat without having to check vending machines for abandoned change to pay for it. She missed the days when hitting a drive thru for a milk shake and fries wouldn't give her pause. Looping around on the lane next to the drive thru, she pulled into a slanted parking spot on the edge of the lot. She gave the cars waiting on their food a couple minutes to pull forward before going inside.

At the counter, she stood far off on the side away from the registers and the line. She waved to get an employee's attention. The man who walked over wore a lighter color uniform shirt, and his name tag read "Shift Supervisor" under his name.

'Perfect.'

"Hi," she said, flashing him a friendly smile. "My boyfriend and I just came through the drive thru, and we didn't get an order of fries."

The employee glanced at the kid working the window, but she was busy collecting a payment. "What size?" he asked Eileen.

"Medium."

"Just one?" He was already on his way to the fry warmer.

"Yeah." She fidgeted nervously worried about being busted.

He unfolded a cardboard box and scooped fries into it, placed it in a bag and brought it to her.

"Thank you," she said before walking out.

His attitude could've been more pleasant. If she was a legitimate paying customer who had been shorted on her order, it would've been barely an inconvenience to go inside to have it fixed. Things happen, and people make mistakes. Had she been met with that gruff attitude after paying, it would have irritated her enough to complain.

She went to her car and opened the bag, inhaling the scent of oil and salt. It had been a long time since she scammed a restaurant out of anything. She told herself it was because she felt bad for stealing. The real reason was she had done it so many times they were beginning to recognize her all over town. This was one of the places she had never hit back then. It was too close to her old life. There was too much of a risk of running into somebody who might recognize her.

The first fry she bit into was still too hot. She fanned her open mouth with her hand trying to cool it off. Somehow she managed to swallow it, and she felt it burn the entire way down her throat. She fished through her book bag for a bottle of water she filled up at home and drank half of it to soothe the burning sensation, wishing the water was colder.

She set the bag between the seats for a few minutes until she could eat them. Ever since dinner with Remus, French fries were all she had been craving. She had forgotten just how delicious they were.

Burger Shack sat on the corner on Pine Street. About a mile down the road was Lake View Lane. The road wrapped around, circling Lovers Lake on the edge of the city. Its official name was Five Lakes. There were several pinches where it narrowed almost cutting it into five separate bodies of water, and did so during droughts, but it was one continuous lake.

No one local called it by its real name. It was an easy way to spot the townies by which name they used. Rumor had it the lake got its name because the area used to be considered a lovers lane of sorts long before her time, before the city expanded and used the scenic border to cater to the rich residents' demand for privacy and pretty views.

Near the end of the lane there were several dead end roads, cul-de-sacs, where the city's most prominent, most elite, most wealthy residents lived. The houses out there were definitely a status symbol. Owning a house there meant hometown legend Billy Tucker might be one of your neighbors.

The lake road was free of cameras, but the side streets were littered with them. She'd attended too many parties out that way to not have seen them perched on all of the houses and driveway gates. She'd have to be invisible to get to Billy Tucker without being caught on someone's security footage.

Once she had her son, she'd be gone, but the death of someone like Tucker would be reported instantly unlike a low life such as Chuck Rogers. She'd be one of the first names on the suspect list for the police to rule out.

'Revenge.'

She reached into the bag and grabbed a fry. They were cooler now and easier to eat. She chewed them slowly, one at a time, trying to savor them.

'If I was going to seek revenge, I'd have done it soon after he killed my boy.'

Eileen stared down the road in the direction of the lake hoping a way to get to him unseen would magically land in her lap. It was too big of a risk. The cops could get to her before her son came to life. They could be detained at the airport. It would be worth it if he was alive, but she wanted to exhaust every option to be there with him first instead of having him visit her in prison. Even if they made it out of the country to someplace without an extraction policy with the States, it would follow them forever. They'd be recognized, taunted, and her son would never get the chance at a normal life he deserved.

It couldn't be at his home. She'd have to find a way to do it while he was out, but following him, learning his schedule would be a risk. Even if it wasn't, he was never alone. Someone like him easily attracted a crowd. She'd have to always be present, always be ready, and wait for the perfect opportunity to present itself. It could take days. Years.

She reached into the bag, but didn't feel anything. The fries were gone, and she sighed. Eating while distracted was a hard habit to break and also a luxury she needed to remember she couldn't afford. She took the cardboard sleeve out of the bag and dumped the last few tiny crumble pieces into her hand. When she tilted her head back to tip them in her mouth, a van caught her attention from the corner of her eye.

It was a white van with swirls of gold shooting off a magic wand. In bright blue letters, the name "Servicella" was written on the side. She recognized the logo and was quite familiar with the company. She had used them for several events many years ago. They were good, the best around, and the price tag on their services reflected that.

'Oh, please.' She begged the universe to let this be the solution she needed.

The van headed north down Pine Street, and she put the car in reverse to follow it. The sound of a horn blaring made her hit her breaks. She hadn't checked to see if there were any cars behind her, and she almost backed right into someone. The man in the pickup truck waved his arms, and she watched his lips move as he yelled at her. She didn't have to hear him to know what he was saying.

Once he passed, she safely backed out of her spot and pulled out onto the road. The van was already out of sight, but there was only one area on this side of the city it could be headed. Eileen drove to Lake View Lane and slowly made her way around the water.

She drove slowly, taking in the scenery, just a regular person enjoying a drive. As she approached the first side street, she became anxious and held her breath. *'Please. Please. Please.'*

The van wasn't anywhere on the street. It was possible it was in a driveway, behind other vehicles, but it was unlikely. People with money rarely did anything to make things easier for those they deemed beneath them.

Eileen drove passed the second and third streets and still no van. Each street increased her heart rate, and she shook nervously until she could see down to the end of the road. Then it all increased for the next one.

There was only one street left: Foxtrot Court. Known as the dancing subdivision, they all had ballroom names. This was where Tucker lived. The street was added specifically for him. His house was the anchor at the very end. The van had to be on this street, and she bit her lip to keep from screaming when she saw it.

Near the end of the road, the van was parked between two houses. Tucker's was one of them. The rear doors were open, and it was already being unloaded. She didn't have time to see which house the carts were pushed into without stopping on the road to watch, and she couldn't attract any attention.

'It has to be him.'

Eileen went to her house in a hurry. She drove around to the back and ran inside. She was filled with excitement and fear and tried to scold herself into calming down until she knew for sure. It might not be Tucker's party.

'He could be invited.'

It had to be at his house. She paced her kitchen floor unable to stay still for a second. She was so close. It was almost over. This was the break she needed, and if it didn't work out, it might be enough for her to lose it.

'Even next door, it could work.'

She tried to stop mid-turn and lost her balance, falling into the island. Both of her hands went out to catch herself, but she barely noticed the pain shooting through her left wrist. The social pages in the paper would have the details. She could easily look to see who was throwing a party.

But, she needed Monday's paper. It was the one day of the week when the social section was printed.

She pressed her fingers to her temples, squeezing her eyes shut, and a steady growl emitted from her pursed lips. There had to be something. Someone. She needed to follow this event.

Her eyes opened wide. The Daily Post. The local paper

had archives available online, and the last two weeks of articles could be searched for free, up to five articles a month without paying for a subscription.

"Internet!" A longer stream of choice words followed. Why hadn't she thought of it before coming home? If Remus hadn't filled her tank, she'd be really hurting.

Eileen ran out of the kitchen, hitting her hip on the door frame when she cut her turn too close, onto the porch and bounded down the steps where she came down on her foot wrong and turned her ankle, and limped toward her SUV. It'd be a miracle if she was able to drive to the nearest free WiFi connection without causing more injury.

She raced down the driveway and halfway to the business district before slowing down and obeying traffic laws. Putting herself on the police radar for any reason wasn't a good idea right now. She pulled into the parking lot of a fast food joint and searched for their network on her phone.

It was taking too long. When it finally pulled up, she hit her steering wheel in frustration waiting on the page to accept their terms and conditions to load. She couldn't type. Her hands were shaking. It took several attempts to get the correct letters for the Daily Post website. She closed out two pop ups, one to log in and the other to pay for a subscription.

In the search box, she began typing, and the website jumped to another screen. "Are you sure? Take 20% off a six week trial if you sign up today. Enter the code SUMMER20 at checkout."

"Ugh!" She looked around to see if anyone was watching her nervous breakdown unfold. There were several cars close to hers, but they were all empty.

She went back to the home page and typed the name Billy Tucker in the little box next to the magnifying glass. The first search turned up nothing which made her heart sink. *'That can't be right. He makes headlines all the time.'*

Either she fat fingered the phone keyboard when she typed his name, or it was a Freudian slip. She found the problem and changed the F to a T. This time the search results yielded pages of articles. She used the filter to list them by date, most recent first.

There it was. "30th Birthday Party for Vanessa Tucker." The article was dated last Monday. Eileen clicked the link. She scanned the page quickly three times without finding the date of the party. It had to be why the Servicella van was on his street. They were the best around at organizing and catering events. *'When is it?'* She screamed inside her head then took a deep breath and actually read most of the entire page out loud on the fourth attempt.

"Summer fling to celebrate... Thirty never looked so good."

'Whatever,' she rolled her eyes. It wasn't Vanessa's fault her husband drove drunk that night she reminded herself.

"Who's who guest list... There! This Friday night."

This was it. This was how she could reach Tucker. The party was tomorrow night which left very little time to prepare.

Eileen dropped her hands to her lap, still clutching the phone. She pulled the visor down and looked in the mirror on the back of it. The face staring at her was still unrecognizable. The dark circles looked more like two black eyes than lack of sleep, poor skin care and an unhealthy diet. She was wrinkled now with deep lines permanently cut into her forehead. There was redness and patches of dry skin she'd been neglecting. A face like this wouldn't get through the door of Tucker's house even without the history they shared.

She put the visor up and drummed the steering wheel with her fingers making a mental list of everything she needed to do within the next twenty-four hours. It was a long list. There wasn't enough time or money to get it all done, but she had to find a way. Tucker was as good as dead once she managed a much needed makeover.

Chapter Nineteen
Coming Home

It had been a difficult night for sleep. In addition to the hard tiled kitchen floor she used for a bed, she was too nervous to drift off. She'd spent the evening devising a plan and knew what she had to do, but it was so far out of character for her.

'It looks good on paper.'

Knowing what needs to be done and actually doing it are two different things.

When the morning light started creeping through the windows chasing away the shadows of the night, it was pointless to continue trying to rest. It would take the better part of the day to get ready for the party at the Tucker house tonight. She was tired, groggy and miserable from the lack of sleep and hoped she'd be more alert by the time she had to act because a second chance might not fall into her lap like this for months.

Her arm was in no shape to drag the pans in to boil water for a bath. After jamming it into the kitchen island the day before, the pain had come back triple fold, and she couldn't afford more pain medication. She went outside to the well with a cup from the kitchen and wet her hair with the freezing cold water, washing it in the yard. It woke her up quicker than anything ever had.

In the bathroom, she used the wet wipes to give herself a bath and tossed the rest of the package in her book bag along with the bracelet. She was clean, but she was far from passing as an event employee. There was one place in town which could help her with everything, and she dreaded going there. She didn't have a choice, and she hoped none of her old acquaintances would be there to recognize her.

Coming Home was a catchall day center that wouldn't exist if it wasn't for her. It provided a place for the homeless community to hang out six days a week. It was closed on Sunday. They had other services available for homeless people and those who had fallen on hard times like help with resume writing and free clothing.

She championed the project, hosting fundraisers, and single handedly brought in over seventy five percent of the money for its construction. The workers were all volunteers except for a few who were employed by an area mental health and substance abuse facility.

When she parked on the street, she didn't go in right away. The screens on the front windows were pulled down preventing the glare of the sun from blinding those inside the building. She couldn't see who was working.

It took almost an hour for her to build the courage to go through the doors. She kept her head down, preparing to bolt if necessary. A man sat behind the desk in the director's office, but he wasn't the same person originally appointed to the role. A few people who looked like staff milled about the open floor plan of the day center, and none of them were familiar to her. She lucked out.

"Hello," a friendly voice called out to her. The young woman was barely an adult, probably a college student working toward a social services or sociology degree. "I haven't seen you here before. Welcome."

Eileen looked around the room, and her heart sank when she didn't see any clothing. There had been racks of it along the back wall the last time she was here which was when the place first opened. It was a long shot, but she'd hoped to find the outfit she needed at Coming Home instead of trying to shoplift it.

"My name's Aubrey. Is there anything I can help you with?" the woman asked.

It was harder admitting to someone else how penniless she was than she thought it would be. The things she did alone were easier. "An outfit," she managed to say.

"Clothes?"

Eileen was certain she was about to say they no longer took clothing donations. "I have a job interview in a few hours," she said, telling the story she concocted last night.

The woman's smile was soft and friendly. "Exciting!"

"A friend told me about this place. I was hoping to find something to wear to the interview."

"Sure. Follow me." Aubrey walked to one of the doors on the side of the room with Eileen at her heels. Through the door were three long rows of clothing. It appeared to be one each for women, men, and children. "What size are you?"

Eileen told her and explained to the woman she had hoped to find a pair of black pants and a white button up shirt specifically. It was the required uniform for the job she was trying to get. Within five minutes, she was headed to the bathroom with three pairs of slacks to try on while Aubrey continued to search for a top.

The first ones she tried fit perfectly, so she didn't bother with the rest. When she came out, she searched the shelves on the wall for shoes. There was a pair of black ballet flats in her size. The old Eileen would cringe over wearing shoes someone else's feet had broken in, but the new version of her was just thankful to find something. Servicella required all of their female servers to wear pumps, but she didn't think anyone would notice. If someone did, it wouldn't matter because she'd be long gone before they could complain about the employee who didn't actually work for them.

"I couldn't find the shirt," Aubrey said, bringing her a handful of others to try.

Eileen took them and went back to the bathroom. She wouldn't be able to wear any of them to the party tonight, but she'd forgotten how great new clothes made her feel until she put on the pants. Even if they weren't brand new, they were new to her. She chose a lightweight rose colored top that looked really good on her and came out, hanging the other two on the rack. Aubrey had disappeared back into the main room.

Shoving her old clothes into the book bag, Eileen headed toward the front door. "Thank you," she said.

"Wait," Aubrey told her. "I just need a few things from you." She was sitting at a bare desk with only a monitor, keyboard and mouse on it.

Eileen took the chair across from her nervously. She didn't think she had to pay.

"We just keep track of the help we provide here," Aubrey explained.

There were a handful of questions about her name, address, and employment status. Aubrey didn't even ask for her ID. Either it was a comfort issue for those who didn't trust easily, or it was an assumption that most homeless people don't have all of their important documents.

"When is your interview?"

"At four," Eileen said. She had created an entire backstory when she couldn't sleep last night. Everything from how she heard about the job and what made her apply, to when and where the interview was to take place had been covered. She even came up with the name of a contact person to ask for when she arrived at the office.

Aubrey looked at her watch. "Plenty of time. Would you like me to do your makeup?"

"My what?" Eileen hadn't expected anything more than clothing.

"Makeup." Aubrey pointed to another part of the room. A small table had been turned into a vanity. It was even equipped with a mirror on the wall. There were many small compacts and tubes on the table she recognized as lipstick and eyeshadow palettes. "You can do it yourself if you like, but I love giving makeovers," Aubrey laughed.

Eileen nodded, but was already on her feet and walking to the table. She sat for about fifteen minutes while Aubrey pulled out various new sponges and cotton swabs out of packages to apply a full face on her. It was the most human, the most reminiscent of her old life, she'd felt in a very long time.

When Aubrey was through, she left Eileen to study her finished look in the mirror. She pulled her brush from the book bag and ran it through her hair, pulling it into a ponytail. A couple of tendrils hung on either side of her face, and she didn't recognize the woman looking back at her. There was the old Eileen whose appearance was always perfect. The recent version of herself was sickly, gaunt, and unkempt. It was the face of a woman who dug through dumpsters for dinner and slept under bridges. This was somebody new. This was someone stuck somewhere in between the other two.

She thanked Aubrey again before leaving, and she stopped her once more. "Don't forget your voucher," she called to Eileen.

"My what?"

Aubrey ran her the slip of paper good for twenty five dollars in merchandise at any of the stores listed. It was like any other coupon and could be used on anything except alcohol and nicotine products. Eileen didn't even have to spend it on clothing. It was about trusting her to use it wisely. "You might not have time before the interview, but it'll get you that shirt after you're hired. And, you *will* get hired," Aubrey smiled and walked back to the desk.

Eileen went outside to her car and looked at the piece of paper in her hand determining which business was closest to her. This was better than she could've hoped. It was like everything was lining up to help her end the life of Billy Tucker, like what she had planned was meant to be.

She left the store with a brand new shirt and had enough to spare to buy a deli sandwich and potato wedges, the next best thing to fast food fries. Her favorite place in the park was occupied, so she drove down Pine Street, parking on the street several blocks from the Burger Shack slowly eating her combination lunch and dinner. Her meal was washed down with the water she brought from home, and she wished she could've got a soda too. She already had to spend ten cents of her own money to cover the difference which was a pretty good deal for all she bought, but ten cents in her world was a fortune.

'It would've just made me sick.' She told herself to feel better about it.

In a few short hours, it would be time to make her move. Everything had to go perfectly. She had to get him alone and get out undetected. The cops would be at her house as soon as his body was discovered, but she wouldn't be there. She'd be at the airport with her son waiting on the first flight out of the country. The rest of the day had gone so smooth, so seamless, and it made her fearful. It had been too easy and better than she anticipated. Something was bound to go very, very wrong tonight.

Chapter Twenty
Showtime

The sun was just beginning to set. The party was underway although most of the guest list wouldn't show up for at least an hour. She made her way toward Foxtrot hoping to get there while there was still a chance to get Tucker alone. How she was going to manage that feat wasn't something she could plan. If an opportunity didn't present itself, she'd just have to act and hope she could get out of there in the mass hysteria and confusion without someone restraining her.

She carefully removed the splint from her arm. It felt fine for a few minutes then a slow throb began in her wrist. She'd have to push through it. A splint on her arm would be too noticeable. Someone might question why she was working, and it would make her stand out from the crowd. People like these didn't give a second thought to those putting in the elbow grease to make their night enjoyable. An employee with a splint would stick in their mind, and they'd be quick to remember her if the police came around asking questions.

The bracelet squealed when she pulled it from the book bag. It hated being confined and begged her to put it on her arm every second she had it tucked safely away. It was another thing which would stand out if she wore it over the long sleeve of her white blouse, but it might ruin a perfect chance, perhaps even her only chance, if she had to wait to undo the buttons at the cuff to roll it up, exposing the bracelet to push the eye to release the dagger.

There was still enough light coming in the windshield for it to reflect off the metal casting a prismatic light show across the ceiling of her car. It was beautiful. Everything about the bracelet was breathtaking. She placed it over her sleeve and clasped it around her arm. When she got to the party, she'd decide whether or not to keep it on.

It was about a mile walk from where she parked her car on the lake road to Billy Tucker's house. It was further to run for her getaway, but less chance of a neighbor blocking the dead end street with their car. Wherever she parked was risky. Her feet wanted to fly her there quickly to get it over and done. The odds of everything going sideways were against her, and she fully believed the night would end with her in handcuffs while her son wandered the cemetery scared and alone. She had to keep slowing herself down because showing up glistening in sweat and out of breath would add to her problems.

The cars parked in a field off the lake road were the only clue a party was underway. The valet company had found a place out of the way to keep the road clear. It was typical of someone like Tucker to go to these extremes instead of renting a suitable venue for the event. *'Or maybe it was something else keeping the party at home?'*

Celebrations and Tucker clearly didn't mix. He joined AA after the accident that took Noah's life, but it was for show. Within months, he was spotted drinking at his usual haunts again, but he had hired a driver.

The Servicella vans were parked past his house in the rounded cul-de-sac end of the road. One of the valets shouted to her as she walked past, teasing her about being late. The outfit worked like she had expected. Music drifted from the backyard. It sounded like a quartet playing soft and slow. Something low enough to not irritate any neighbors who weren't coming, or worse, weren't invited.

She tried the door of the first one she came to, and it was unlocked. There was an apron hanging from a hook in the back of the van which she put on. It had a name tag attached to it, Brandi. There was a large front pocket, and she slipped the bracelet off her wrist and dropped it inside. It immediately begged her to wear it. The cries from the pocket grew louder the longer she ignored it.

Walking toward the house, her body was tensed, waiting for someone to appear at any moment asking questions. Who are you? Where's your ID? You're not on their employee list? I already checked Brandi in. Did you leave, and did you have permission? No one was around except for two men standing at a podium at the end of the circle drive waiting to park guests' cars. They barely noticed her aside from their initial greeting.

Two Servicella employees came from the side of the house. Eileen kept her head down until they passed. They were complaining about being sent on break so early when there was still so much time left in their shifts. The manager wanted everyone on the floor when the party was in full swing until it started dying down hours from now.

Eileen went in the direction they had emerged and walked along the house to the backyard. The side gate was open, and she walked into the party unnoticed. Guests would come in the front door, take in the lavish décor and vast expense of Tucker's home then enter the party from the rear of the house.

The home was gorgeous and worth a pretty penny. If he hadn't ended his career so early, he and his wife would have probably moved out of state, ended up in a mansion on acres and acres of land. They were stuck here now. He was a big fish in a small pond and enjoyed the celebrity attention from the locals. His money lasted longer in a place like this.

She walked to the bar set up across the yard and grabbed an empty tray, giving the bartender a fake drink order. Once the tray was loaded, she walked through the party, pretending to work even collecting a few empty glasses people placed on the tray as she passed.

When she saw him, he was in the middle of a large group of people. Vanessa was nowhere in sight. *'Probably preparing to make an entrance once most of the guest list had arrived.'*

Forget the getaway. It would be impossible to get to him right now. Once someone saw her as she approached, she'd be recognized. No one was giving a second thought to a waitress, but if that lowly employee was coming close to them, they'd pay attention. She'd have to wait until the crowd was too large to be bothered with an individual, until there was a distraction like someone on stage wishing Vanessa a happy birthday.

Tensions had been strained between the two of them since the accident. Not because he struck down and killed a ten year old boy. Oh, no. She stuck by her husband's side through all of the initial negative press like his own personal public relations guru. The accident was blamed on the old bridge. It was designed poorly for the growing city, not giving pedestrians room to safely cross. The road wasn't well lit which was dangerous given the curves. And, Eileen's favorite, what was a boy so young doing out that late by himself? Where were his parents?

'It was my fault,' she blinked back tears. *'That's why I'm*

going to fix my mistake.'

Their marital problems came in the months after the news coverage settled down, and the trial was over. Time served – a whole three days, a fine, attend AA meetings for three months which was waived because he was already in the program, and community service. The work he already did around the community would count toward his hours. Tucker was done paying for his crime in a matter of weeks.

The baby they lost that night would always haunt him. Eileen didn't break from her old life immediately. She had friends until she pulled away for Noah's sake. They kept her informed of the Tucker gossip whether she wanted to hear it or not. Every juicy detail Vanessa shared in confidence found its way to Eileen's ears. They were hurting over a baby they never got to meet, to hold, to name. The baby had only existed in positive blood tests. Somehow people thought their pain was on par with hers. What they went through wasn't even close to the nightmare she was trapped repeating every day.

He was supposed to be home that night, but he let his wife down in more ways than one. Vanessa didn't go to the party because she didn't want anyone to notice she wasn't drinking. It was still early days of the pregnancy, and she didn't want to share the news until after the first trimester. It had been assumed Billy would stay home with her.

When he didn't, a very irritated Vanessa went on a shopping spree courtesy of her husband's credit cards. She carried her bags upstairs easily enough, but a dress bag caught under her heal causing her to lose her balance near the top of the main staircase before the landing. In trying to save herself from tumbling down backward, she overcorrected and went over the rail landing on the cold Italian tile of the foyer.

Her first call was to Billy who left the party immediately and sped home. He took the roads around the city thinking it'd save time in traffic. She laid there for over an hour in pain while she miscarried, waiting on the man who'd never come because he was tied up with the police and a situation of his own. When she finally called an ambulance, she went to the hospital, learned the tragic news and came home alone.

It's something that'd be hard for anyone to forgive.

The din of voices around Eileen grew louder as she came out of her thoughts. She'd been staring off in a daze of remembered conversations and would soon draw unwanted attention if she didn't get back to work. There was an empty table near the gardens, and she set the tray on it as she walked by.

Hired hands, Servicella employees and others, were coming and going through the backdoor. There was apparently work to be done inside. People like Tucker didn't allow the help to use their facilities, so it couldn't be that. That's why there were portable toilets in the field near the lake. The event staff were covered although it was quite a hike if they were in a hurry, and it wasn't an eye sore for the residents.

She was just about to the back door when two servers dressed almost identically to her came out. "These are the last of the hors d'oeuvres," one said.

"It'll be fifteen minutes before more are ready," said the second.

They were trying to deter her from going inside. More help was needed in the yard, passing drinks and collecting empty glasses. Eileen didn't hesitate and kept walking toward the house. The kitchen was to the right, but she bee lined straight ahead.

She'd been here once many years ago. It was right after his medical release from his knee injury. Tucker was drafted, bought this house, played a few games then was benched the rest of the season and never played again. He thought his release meant he'd rejoin the team and be ready for next season. The kid was a whiz with a basketball, but dumb when it came to anything else. He was medically released alright. His treatments were done, but he'd never be able to play the sport professionally again.

The richest tier of the elite celebrated that night. They cheered him on. Rooted for him in his career. Two days later the headlines ran a completely different story. Billy Tucker was benched permanently.

It'd been years ago, and she didn't sneak off to explore the house. She remembered very little except there was a hall closet behind the stairs in the foyer. It's where her jacket had been hung that night. She crept down the hallway from the rear until she saw it. The closet was roomy enough for her and several others to hide out. She pulled the two sliding doors shut leaving just enough of a gap to see though.

The bracelet wanted her to be prepared. It reminded her every second she hesitated increased her odds of failure. Eileen listened to it, and secured it on her right wrist. Even in the almost pitch black darkness of the closet, she could sense its gleam.

Eileen was so entranced by the allure of the Egyptian eye she almost missed it when Billy Tucker walked down the hallway passed the closet where she was hiding. This was too good to be true. She expected to have to wait for at least a couple hours until the party was in full swing before going outside to find her target. There'd be less chance of being found out as an imposter if she stayed away as long as possible. It was another sign she was on the right path.

She opened the door slowly and looked around. There was no one in the hall, but she could hear footsteps above her. He was going upstairs. She went quickly, keeping an eye on him, not wanting to get too close yet. Part of her worried he had come in to fetch the birthday girl. There was something about stabbing him in a crowd that was less unsettling than killing him in front of his wife alone.

At the landing, she went left like she'd seen him do. She barely made it to the top of the stairs in time to see which room he ducked into, and she hurried down to it. Her heart banged against the inside of her chest so hard it pained her with each dramatic beat. She was shaking and scared. Tucker was more physically fit than the last two men she overpowered combined.

The door to the bedroom was cracked, and she saw him sitting on the edge of the bed. He was bent over with his elbows on his legs and his head hung down. He looked upset about something not that she really cared why.

This room was small. It wasn't anything like what she would imagine their bedroom to look like if she'd given it much thought. The room was barely larger than her sons. The décor was masculine and plain. This wasn't a couple's room. There was no feminine touch to it. No brush or lotion on the nightstand. No robe draped over a chair. Nothing in this room belonged to Vanessa. The talk around town had been right.

They were having problems, and it appeared they had separate bedrooms to go with it.

Eileen was halfway to the bed lost in her thoughts again before she realized she'd entered the room. It was her gasp when reality flooded back into her mind that caught Billy's attention and alerted him to her presence. She panicked and pressed the eye, releasing the blade. With her hand curled into a fist and tucked down to her wrist, she ran toward him.

He straightened and turned in her direction. His eyes widened at the madwoman coming for him. He opened his mouth and raised his hands to grab her, to fight her off. As he lifted off the bed, he saw her, really saw her. The apprehension in his eyes was replaced with a peaceful surrender. "It's you," he said, dropping back to the bed. His gaze fell to the floor again, allowing her to do what she must.

The blade went into his neck easy, and she yanked her arm to the side, wanting to pull it across the front of his throat. It barely moved. She grabbed it with her left hand to add more force, but a sharp pain cut through her wrist sending a current of aftershocks up her arm. She cried out a low whimper, but he remained silent.

Eileen stabbed him multiple times in the neck, and he fell to the floor. The blood pouring from his wounds spilled out onto the rug in an almost black puddle. He didn't fight her off. He didn't try to scream. The only sound coming from Billy was a gargling noise as he choked on the blood pouring from his neck.

All the life had drained from his eyes before Eileen was willing to leave. This had to be it. He took her son's life, and she took his. An eye for an eye. It's what the dagger demanded. The news would later say Tucker's murderer gouged out one of his eyes, but she had no memory of that. She could've swore both eyes were open, blankly staring at nothing when she left him dead on the floor.

So far everything had gone smoothly. His body could be discovered at any time, even while she was still in the room. Once the alarms were sounded, it would be more difficult for Eileen to escape.

She backed away from the body as if it might jump up at any moment to attack her, as if it was waiting for her to let her guard down. When she reached the door, she left the room without checking to see if the coast was clear. She locked the door before pulling it shut. It might buy her a little time if it was assumed he wanted some privacy. Eventually, they'd find a way in to check on him. Tucker wouldn't miss his own wife's big night.

There was only one valet at the podium when she strutted right out the front door. The other she assumed was parking a car. The one who was several yards in front of her was busy on his phone, and didn't see her until after she walked by. He yelled something at her she didn't quite catch, so she flashed him the peace sign without looking back.

Once she rounded the corner where the driveway met the sidewalk and turned toward the lake road, she was scot-free. She strolled down the street, taking her time. It was a beautiful night. No need to rush now that her business had been tended, forgetting the cops could be behind her at any moment tracking her down. She made it to the car and climbed in the driver's seat. The bracelet shone in the moonlight. There were specks of blood dirtying its beauty. She'd clean it again when she took it off.

Right now, it deserved to be showcased proudly. It had earned its freedom for the evening, and she wasn't going to take that away from it.

Chapter Twenty-One
Waiting in Vain

Eileen drove straight to the cemetery. This time she didn't slow down to check for movement on her way to the small opening in the trees less than a mile north of it where she hid her car. Her wrist was throbbing, screaming at her to stop and at least find some cheap over the counter something or another for pain, but it was background noise. She was sharply focused on getting Noah.

This time it had to work. Take the life of the person responsible. That's what Remus had said or something along those lines. An eye for an eye. It made perfect sense, and she kicked herself for not thinking about it herself sooner. At one point, Tucker was on her short list of people to go after with the dagger.

'At one point? More like always.' There was no short list. He *was* the list.

The only thing that stopped her was she'd be the number one suspect if something happened to him. *'When something happened.'* It was already done. *'When his body is discovered.'*

Well, that and it being hard to get close to him with his celebrity status and their history. Tonight had been laid out perfectly on a silver platter for her. It was meant to be. There was no other explanation for it. She'd still be the first one the police wanted to question, but they'd go to her house and find it empty because she'd be waiting at the gate for her flight with her son at her side.

She played with her bracelet, pushing the eye over and over. Push the eye, and the dagger releases. Push it again, and the dagger retracts. The mom voice in her head scolded her. *Don't play with the button like that or you'll break it.*

The dagger didn't mind. It enjoyed being wanted. She hated the thought of taking it off now. She liked how she felt wearing it and how the bracelet made her feel about herself even if that person was a murderer. It made her feel confident like she was finally in charge of her life again. It belonged on her wrist forever, and she wondered if airport security would detect the blade hidden within.

No, she was supposed to give it to Remus before she left the country. That was the deal.

'I could always mail it to myself overseas.' She wondered how that could work since she didn't have a permanent address, but she could mail it to their hotel if she was able to get to a post office before heading to the airport. She'd figure it out. She always did. Remus wouldn't be able to stop her. He wouldn't even know she had gone.

She walked the path up to the brick wall quickly. The large rock was waiting for her, ready to help boost her over. She put one foot on it and reached up to the ledge with both hands. The moment she put pressure on her wrist, a pain seared up her arm, and she fell to the ground.

The ground was soft and littered with small twigs and other debris from the trees. With a clear mind, she would've been thankful it hadn't rained recently, but in her current state, she didn't even give the bits of dirt and grass clinging to her a second thought. She rolled around, gripping her arm above the wrist, above the pain. The splint was still in her car where she took it off earlier, but it was too late to go back for it.

It wasn't really too late. She was on no one's timeframe but her own. She didn't want to double back. Noah was on the other side of this wall somewhere in the darkness looking for her, and she wasn't going to make him wait one minute longer than was absolutely necessary.

Eileen rolled on to her knees and stood up keeping her left arm folded tightly across her body. She went back to the wall and managed to pull herself up with one hand. Barely, but she made it.

It was awkward and her movements were clumsy, but she sat up on the ledge. Before throwing herself onto the ground below, she looked at the mausoleum filled with hope only to feel the shattering heartache she'd grown accustomed to experiencing since the accident. The moon was full, and it glimmered off the chain laced through the doors, hanging where she had left it after cutting through one of the links. Her son was still inside.

The chain hung in two large sections, and she was surprised the groundskeepers hadn't noticed it yet. They wouldn't have a reason to go into the mausoleum necessarily, but they're around it weekly, if not almost daily. The mowing and other landscaping, tending to other graves, and any other work they're responsible for had them working right alongside the building.

Once the bracelet was found, she hadn't expected it'd take this long to be reunited with Noah. Leaving the busted chain that first night was a little worrisome, but she hadn't given it a lot of thought since then. Any one of these nights recently she could've shown up to find a new chain had been strung through the door to replace it. During any one of the days since the bridge the cops could've swung by her house to ask about it, wondering if she was up to her old tricks again.

Under different circumstances, she'd complain. Her son wasn't being properly cared for during his rest. They weren't doing their jobs well. The eye to detail of the cemetery staff left a lot to be desired. Doing so now would out her nocturnal activities in the process.

She was under the belief she had chosen the best cemetery in the city for her son, but it was no different than the rest. People don't care about the dead. Even loved ones typically stop visiting after a little while. It's too far out of the way. It's too hot, too cold. The hours are inconvenient. There's always an excuse, and then they stop making those as well as the visits.

Once again, she stayed on the wall waiting for something to happen. Her ears deciphered every noise from the breeze in the trees to the scurry of a small animal, listening for the sound of her son's voice. Her eyes trained on the entrance to the mausoleum longing to see it open, watching for the chain to move from the slightest sway of the doors.

There was little emotion. What little hope she had left when she saw the chain hanging down in the same place it was the last time she was here. There was no anxiety or agitation, no worry or concern, no fear or excitement. She wasn't filled with anticipation over whether her son was going to walk out of that mausoleum into the night because he was. He had to. Eileen didn't feel any guilt over anything she had done whether during the last week or the previous two years to get Noah back.

She wasn't worried if someone recognized her at the party or worried the cops would link it back to her. She didn't even overthink what she'd do if she went home tonight, without Noah yet again, and the police showed up to take her in for Tucker's murder. The cops were going to question her without a doubt. She might not be number one on the list of suspects. They always rule out the spouse first, don't they? But, she was definitely near the top.

She was completely numb. Aside from the sharp throbs of pain shooting from her wrist up her arm, she felt absolutely nothing.

Noah was going to come to life. He would make it. He had to. If he didn't, there was no reason for her to continue.

As time passed, she thought about everything and nothing. The question she often bounced around in her head was what she would do with her son first, but tonight it dawned on her that it wasn't optional. They'd have to flee the country first. Eventually, the murders would be linked to her somehow, and her son's sudden reappearance would raise a lot of eyebrows. She wouldn't be able to take him to the campsites, theme parks, and ball games that kept popping into her mind. The first thing they'd do is leave the country, but once they were safe, they could figure out together what they'd do first in their new home.

His second chance at life couldn't be explained away. No one would believe the dagger was capable of resurrection. If she allowed herself to dwell on that topic for even a minute, she'd suspect she wasn't entirely positive it was possible anymore either. If she did manage to convince anyone, she'd only be admitting her own guilt in the process.

Eileen was exhausted. She laid on the wall with her head on her left shoulder, stretching her arm across the ledge. The throbbing was still there and grew worse in this position, but she ignored it. This was the only way she could admire the dagger. For minutes, for hours, she had no way to gauge how much time had passed, but she laid there staring at the bracelet admiring its beauty. Every time she blinked she noticed something new in the design, some new speck of color or minute detail she hadn't previously noticed. It was a shame she'd neglected it for so long. A rare piece of history like this with so much power deserved better.

She pressed the eye and watched the dagger release. Most of the blade shimmered inches from her face except where Tucker's blood muddied it, blocking the reflection of the light. "I'm so sorry," she said, feeling remorse for not cleaning it right away.

This should've been a priority. It was wrong of her to treat the bracelet this way. She might not have need to use it again, but that was no excuse to abuse it. The search for and purchase of this dagger cost her the bulk of her fortune. It was worth more money than the average person could fathom, and she had to make sure it was kept in good condition.

She removed the bracelet and wiped the blade on her pants. It caught in the fabric, and she felt it cut a small hole. The pants were temporary anyway and not her style. They were only needed to serve the purpose of passing for catering staff at the party. When she examined the blade again, it hadn't made much of a difference because the blood had dried. It had to be cleaned. That was most pressing right now.

She sat up on the ledge, defeated once more and swung her legs around to dangle over the backside of the wall. It was time to go. She wanted to be long gone before any of the living turned up at the cemetery.

It hadn't worked this time either. Noah was still dead. He wasn't going to be walking out of the mausoleum tonight, or tomorrow, or any other night before Remus finally figured out what the ancient script on the sides of the gauntlet meant. She wasn't sure exactly when she realized tonight wasn't the night, but just before the sunrise broke over the horizon, when the sky turned a lighter monochrome shade of blue, she knew it was time to leave.

Chapter Twenty-Two
Hello, Officer

There on the passenger side of her car was the apron she had torn off when she left the party. She sighed remembering she had to get rid of it. There was always something to clean, something to toss, something to hide after every use of the dagger. It was tiring, and she wasn't done yet because Noah was still dead.

The apron half covered the splint she had left behind when she went to the party. She placed it on her left wrist and lower arm, strapping it tightly. The pressure and support eased one pain and created two more. It felt better with it off, but she was only making it worse.

Eileen glanced at the wall which she could see clearer now as the sky brightened around her. Another night. Another failure. She was leaving the cemetery alone, and the only thing she felt was nothing. There was no sadness, longing, or regret. She'd clean up and rest then plan her next move.

She backed onto the road and went to the nearest gas station not caring which one it was. Her exhaustion ran too deep to concern herself with what businesses and traffic lights might have cameras attached to them and whether or not the police could track her.

She pulled up to a pump without any regard to the other vehicles getting fuel. If she had the good sense to concern herself with who might be around, she wouldn't have stopped. Shouldn't have stopped. What she should, would and did had been blurring for some time.

Her tank was still almost full, but she opened the fuel door and inserted the nozzle anyway. She checked the plastic tubbed screwed to the side of the island. It wasn't the clearest, but at least it wasn't empty. She shook the excess liquid off the windshield squeegee and cleaned her windows. Still wearing the bracelet.

This was another one of her tricks. If the clerk believed she might buy gas, she'd be left alone. There'd only been one time a clerk ran out to yell at her. "That's for paying customers *only*!" But once was enough.

After she cleaned up her car, she moved it to the side of the building. It almost hurt her to take off the bracelet. The emotions stirred up from removing it were strong enough she felt an imaginary physical twinge shoot through her arm. She turned it over in her hands, pressed the eye, and stared at the dagger astonished by it. The entire piece was beautiful, yet it was so simple in concept really.

Using a baby wipe, she cleaned off the blade of the dagger and dug in to the nooks and crannies of the decorative gauntlet as best she could. The blood had dried, and it was going to take a more thorough cleaning than she could manage in the front seat of her car at daybreak. She wouldn't be able to do right by it until she got home.

She wrapped the apron around the bloody wipe and carried it to the dumpster ten to fifteen feet from where she parked, ignoring the dark smears on the passenger seat where the blood had transferred off the black fabric of the Servicella apron. The first hint of sunrise was peaking over the horizon when she tossed the blood covered evidence. A large sign hung from the fence surrounding the dumpster alerting customers it was for gas station use only. A second sign read, "Smile!" There was a picture of a security camera underneath the one word warning. It was almost identical to the one mounted on the wall of the gas station pointed directly at the dumpster. Eileen saw all of it and didn't care.

She walked to the back of the SUV, opened her duffle bag, and pulled out a twenty dollar bill from her secret stash of cash. The change leftover from the night she went to dinner with Remus was in the center console, but she was going to need more than a handful of small silver coins. She did it quickly not allowing herself to second guess her decision because she hated to spend a penny of it. This was meant for when her son returned. It was money to help them start over again in a new land. She wasn't sure she could find something to sell to replace it.

The sign for the restrooms was hanging above a hallway in the back of the small convenience store. She headed there first. As she approached, she saw the police officer standing at the coffee station. His car had been parked at a pump in the fuel island when she pulled onto the lot, and she barely noticed anyone else was there at all. Even this close to him she didn't pay attention to the uniform he wore until she hesitated looking at the coffee and various flavorings available. She didn't expect the gas station to serve the world's finest cup of joe, but it had been a long time since she had anything besides truck stop brew.

The police officer, probably getting that off putting sensation someone was watching him, looked her way and gave a slight nod. His eyes searched her face, scanned her body down to her feet and back again.

Eileen smiled at him weakly. "Evening," she said. The front of his uniform featured his badge on one side, and a small name plate on the other which read, "E. Clemmons." She wondered if the E stood for Edward. He didn't look like an Emmett or Eugene.

"Morning," he countered, smiling at her.

His voice shook her away from the deliberation over his name. She considered his reply carefully, confused at first since she had been distracted by her thoughts again. She glanced out the tall windows along the front of the building at the early dawn light brightening everything more and more by the second. "Yeah," she finally said. "Good morning."

"Hard night?" the cop asked. He lifted his coffee cup to his mouth and took a sip, screwing up his face in disapproval. Before setting the cup down to add more sugar, he pointed toward her blouse.

"You have no idea," she said. Eileen looked down and didn't see anything at first. Then she saw the splatters of dried blood on either side of her shirt. It was old and no longer the vibrant red hue it would've been when it first sprayed across her. It could be anything really not just blood. In her old life, the shirt would look as good as new by the end of the day, but she wouldn't be able to remove the stains with the conditions she was living in at home. It disgusted her more to see the shirt ruined then it did to realize she'd been wearing another man's blood all night long. The shirt was only needed for the party, but she still hated to see it wasted.

"I guess aprons don't protect from everything," she thought out loud. She had believed the apron was the only thing dirtied in the attack on Tucker. It never occurred to her to be concerned a police officer was staring at evidence of murder when he looked at her.

The cop chuckled, and said, "Yeah, I've had those kinds of nights myself."

"I bet you have," she smiled. "I only had drunks throwing food and drinks around to deal with though."

"You know," the officer said, replacing the lid on his coffee. "I had to deal with that last night too."

Eileen grinned wondering if he was at the same party, and understanding she was the reason he'd been there if he was. "Have a good day," she said, and walked away, hearing the cop wish her the same as she left.

She went to the women's restroom. There were three stalls, but she still locked the door behind her. She slipped off the splint and the bracelet, setting them on either side of one of the sinks. When she stood at the basin washing her hands carefully as the pain in her left wrist almost had her in tears, she saw the reflection of the aged and broken version of herself in the mirror.

It wasn't just her shirt covered with blood. Her face had been hit as well. Some of it had been smeared before it had a chance to dry leaving brownish rust colored streaks on her cheeks. She was a walking advertisement for a murder suspect. Her makeup which had previously made her feel good, reminding herself of the old days, had become atrocious. A mix of blood, sweat and time had taken its toll.

She wet a few paper towels and used the hand soap to wash her face completely clean. There were no traces of blood or makeup left except for the blackened lines of residual eyeliner and mascara she couldn't erase no matter how many times she wiped it away.

At this hour, the gas station wouldn't have too many customers. She took advantage of it by using more paper towels to wash up what she could at the sink where there was plenty of light and running hot water. It was hard to undo the button on the cuff of her shirt. The only way to remove the shirt later might be to cut it off.

Her arm was swollen down into her palm. In the darkness of the car, she hadn't seen how much worse it had gotten. She rolled the sleeve up and admired the varying shades of bruising on her arm. Some of it was green and yellow where the bruises were clearing up. Other spots were fresh, a deep purple, and it was proof she'd been injuring it more.

She replaced the splint and turned her attention to the bracelet. Most of the time she spent in the restroom was trying to clean it better than the baby wipe had managed. It wasn't enough. It deserved more. Better. It would have to wait until she was home and could use the peroxide on it.

When she finally left the bathroom, the police officer was gone. She scanned the store, but didn't see him. She stopped at the coffee station and fixed herself a tall cup of black coffee. On her way to the register, she grabbed several packages of over the counter pain medication. That was the whole reason she came inside in the first place.

The officer's car was still at the pump when she walked around the corner of the building. He was sitting in his car, and it looked like he was having some sort of conversation through the radio he wore. She continued to her car, rehearsing lines in her head.

"No, officer. That's not my apron. My name's Eileen. I don't even know a Brandi." She'd show him her license to prove it.

"I didn't see anyone around the dumpster when I pulled in."

"Yes, that's my vehicle, but I haven't been to the Five Lakes area in years."

By the time she got in her car, Officer Clemmons had driven off. He wasn't waiting on her, or checking if her or her vehicle matched an eye witness account after all. She set her coffee in the cup holder and pulled through the rows of pumps on her way to the side street. Her smile grew wider with each security camera she passed.

The packages of pain medicine she purchased were a hard plastic case containing two packets of pills in each one. She couldn't tear them open with two good hands. Her coffee was too hot to take pills yet anyway. She found something in her kitchen to cut them open when she got to the house and took two extra strength acetaminophen and two ibuprofen at once. There was enough left for a few more doses just like that. She hoped it worked because the pain was becoming unbearable.

She sprayed the bracelet with peroxide and scrubbed it with her toothbrush. She was exhausted, but she wouldn't be able to sleep if the dagger hadn't been cared for properly. She laid down on the cold hard kitchen floor hoping the pain medication would kick in soon so she could rest.

The dagger had been on her wrist, but every time she moved, it clanged loudly on the tile. She didn't want to hurt it and could hear it moaning from every bump and bruise she gave it. She took it off and hugged it to her chest, cuddling it like she did her stuffed animals when she was a child.

Chapter Twenty-Three
Unexpected Visitors

Eileen tilted her head to the side trying to figure it out. It was a sound she almost recognized, but she couldn't quite place it. This old house had more than its fair share of creaks and groans. Every sigh of these old wooden bones could be heard crisply without the hustle of a lived in household. There were no televisions, radios or phones to fill in the deadness of the silence. No longer was there a child's laughter or incessant rambling about anything that crossed his mind. There was no movement throughout the house by anyone except her, and she kept mostly to the kitchen.

She lay on her back on the cold tile floor where she'd been for hours. In her hands, she held the gauntlet. The dagger was released, and she was admiring the shine on the blade. It had taken her hours of scrubbing to return its former glory. The bracelet was happy with her work; it had told her so. The bracelet enjoyed being admired by her.

It had been on her wrist, but it was too hard to press the eye to release the dagger with the fingers on her left hand. The pills from the convenience store were helping, but it took three doses to see any real improvement in her pain. The force required to press the eye sent shockwaves of pain through her arm and brought tears to her eyes. She had to hold the bracelet instead of wearing it if she wanted to appreciate it fully.

The sound returned. It reminded her of something she couldn't put her finger on yet. It was something from a busier time from a life she barely recognized as her own. Maybe it wasn't even real. She had been daydreaming, about what she couldn't recall, but it might have been a thought brought to life for one moment.

Then she heard it again. Someone was at the door. It wasn't a knock so much as a pounding. The only person it could be was Remus. No one else knew she still lived in this abandoned home except her ex-husband. He wouldn't come by for any reason. In fact, Eileen was fairly positive he'd give up his life before having to come face to face with her again.

She made her way to the door wishing she knew what Remus wanted before answering him. Her cell phone was dead. All attempts he would've made to get ahold of her before making the drive out here would have been in vain. If she had charged it this morning as had been her plan, she could've avoided having to put on a friendly face and entertaining him for a while.

A few feet from the door, the pounding returned. "Hold your horses!" she yelled. "I'm coming!" She slipped the bracelet into the pocket of her robe. She was certain Remus wouldn't take it from her. If that was his intention, he'd have tried by now, but it was a risk she didn't want to take.

With her hand on the door knob, she slipped deeper into confusion. *'The padlocks,'* she thought. For a second, she began to turn around and head out back, but then the details of last night and this morning came back slowly at first before flooding her mind. The door wasn't locked at all, not even from the inside.

Why had she come in the front door? It was easier and much faster to drive around back and come inside. There was only one lock on the back door compared to the four padlocks on this one. It had been a long night. She hadn't been thinking straight when she came home.

Eileen shook her head at her own stupidity. Behavior like this was exactly why she would wind up behind bars instead of starting over in another country, happily living the rest of her life reunited with her son. She took a deep breath and stretched out her neck, but she couldn't force a smile.

Swinging the door open, a smile crept across her face when she saw who the visitors were. This was an unexpected surprise. Four uniformed officers stood in front of her. Two were near the front step, another stood beside one of the two squad cars parked on either side of her SUV, and the other used his hands to shield the light around his face while he looked in the rear windows of her car. There were two other men in suits directly in front of her on the stoop. An unmarked sedan was parked in the lane.

'Detectives,' she thought.

It was bound to happen eventually. She knew she was living free on borrowed time ever since the night beneath the bridge. The curiosity began to build as to which murder they were here to arrest her for committing.

"Eileen McBride?" the first detective asked.

She nodded, "Yeah." The two police officers near the door stood with faces frozen like statues. Neither was the one she had met at the gas station. *'What was his name? Eddie?'*

"I'm Detective Larson," he said, flashing his badge at her. "This is my partner Detective Woods."

She glanced at the other man, but didn't say anything. Her attention went back to the officer peering through the windows of her SUV. If he was looking for a murder weapon, he'd never find it even if it was right in front of his face. The smile tried to form again, but she bit the inside of her cheek to stop it. Her hand moved across the fabric of the robe, feeling the gauntlet hidden inside.

The uniformed officer standing next to the patrol car wasn't Eddie either, but this man at the SUV could be him. She wasn't able to see his face clearly. *'Not Eddie. His name began with an E. It might be Elliot.'*

"We're sorry to bother you like this, ma'am," Larson continued.

"What's he doing?" Eileen asked, nodding in the direction of her car.

Detective Woods called out to the officer to stop. The nosy cop walked over to join the other uniformed officer by the squad car.

She was still watching him walk away from her car when Larson spoke again. "Mrs. McBride, I'm sure you have an idea of why we're here."

The last officer wasn't E. Clemmons either. It deflated her, hoping to see a friendly face. She wondered if he would remember her, if he would recognize her without all the makeup covering the toll her grief and stress had taken on her features. *'He might remember your blood splattered face and shirt,'* she smiled. That would be a fun game to play.

"Not at all," she replied. Eileen swept her eyes over all the officers. "I keep to myself, so seeing all of you here is actually quite alarming."

She was too calm. Like their visit was expected. "If something happened to my ex-husband, forgive me for not appearing upset. He is my ex for a reason."

"No, ma'am," Larson nodded. "You haven't seen or heard the news this weekend then? Nothing at all?"

"Don't watch it usually." She no longer owned a television set and didn't have the electricity to run one. No cable to watch anything if she did. The truck stop diner and the laundromat were the only places she was able to watch, and it wasn't her controlling the remote when she did. "Why? What happened? Why are you here?"

He turned to his partner, and they exchanged a look. "This is just a standard visit," Woods began. "William Tucker was found dead two nights ago."

Eileen's head whipped toward him fast and hard enough she felt the muscle pull. It would be a literal pain in the neck for her to deal with for a few days now. "What?" she asked in shock.

The surprise was genuine. *It had been two nights ago?* Eileen's thoughts raced, but she was almost certain she had heard the detective correctly. It went without saying she hadn't been herself lately. Losing track of time was common when your life held nothing but emptiness, but she had never misplaced an entire day before.

What had she done besides sleep on the kitchen floor and clean the bracelet. Not much. Had she slept an entire day away? Had she really been that drained?

"Murdered," Larson added.

There were so many thoughts running through her mind. Mostly, she wondered what they meant by a standard visit and how they found out it was her so soon. It had been years since Noah died. If all she wanted was to avenge his death, she'd have killed Tucker sooner.

There would be tricks. This was a game all investigators played to their advantage. They gave out false information or kept some details tight lipped to draw out the suspect. She wouldn't fall into any trap they were trying to set. She was smarter than the average criminal. She would keep her mouth shut.

"We would like to ask you a few questions," Larson continued. "It's procedural. Given the history," Larson's voice trailed off. "We just need to rule you out as a suspect."

Eileen nodded even though she wasn't in agreement with what he was saying. Aside from a few interviews right after her son's death, there had never been any ill will coming from her end. The evil thoughts she had about that man were kept to herself. The public took his side from the moment the metal of his car shrieked as it crumpled on the bridge. He was a golden boy who could do no wrong even when a child lay dead in the street. Every word from her mouth alienated her even more from a city that managed to paint him a victim in the lawsuits filed against him. There was no reason to suspect her. The spouse is supposed to be the primary suspect. That's what all the crime shows would lead one to believe.

"Mrs. McBride?" Larson asked.

She hadn't realized he had said anything else to her. "I'm sorry. I'm trying to figure out how I feel about this news."

"That's understandable," Woods chimed in. "So may we come in?"

"What?" she asked.

"To talk to you? May we come in?" Woods asked as if he had already repeated the question several times.

Eileen was still in the doorway, and she instinctively pulled the door to her, narrowing the opening. The clothes she had worn to the party were still in the kitchen covered in blood. She had never burned them like she planned that night. "I'd rather you not. The house is a mess. Can't we do this outside?"

"No need," Larson held up a hand. "If you'd like you can come down to the station later after you've had time to freshen up," he said.

She glanced down at the robe she was wearing over a worn t-shirt and nothing else. It made her feel suddenly uncomfortable realizing how visible she was to these men standing before her. She grabbed the open sides of the robe and pulled them tightly around her.

When she returned her attention to the detectives, she noticed Larson was staring at the splint on her left hand.

"What happened there?" he asked, pointing to her arm.

"I fell," she said.

"When?" Woods asked.

"About a week ago," Eileen answered. She tried to do the math in her head, but it was hard when she wasn't sure what day it was. How many days had actually passed since she visited the clinic? If she lost a day since Tucker's murder, there might be other days that were missing too.

"Hmm," Larson squinted his eyes and tilted his head while studying the brace. "Bad sprain?" he asked, lifting his eyes to meet her.

"No. It's broke."

"And there are doctor's records then? To prove this happened last week?" Woods inquired.

"Yeah, at the clinic." She fished through the pockets of the robe with her right hand, having to reach across her body for the left side pocket until her fingers brushed against the pill bottle. "This is the prescription they gave me that day," she said, handing him the bottle. The date would be on it even if she couldn't say for certain how long ago it was.

Woods looked the bottle over and handed it back. He turned to Larson and nodded. The two detectives exchanged a glance that clearly said there was no way she overpowered a professional athlete with a broken arm.

Eileen fought back another grin. They didn't know her very well at all.

"When can we expect you then?" Larson asked her as his partner walked away, updating the officers.

Eileen exhaled loudly and said, "I don't know." She didn't even know what time it was now. She couldn't guess a time she'd come to the station if her freedom depended on it. "A few hours." She held up her left hand, showing off the splint again. "It takes me longer to do anything with this bum wrist."

Larson furrowed his brows and looked away. He screwed up his mouth and kicked a stone off her steps. "That's fine. Take all the time you need." He nodded at her and walked to the unmarked car.

She closed the door and walked back to the kitchen. She walked past the pile of clothes on the floor she had worn to the party. The shirt lay on top with the almost black markings of dried blood clearly visible. She walked past the counter where the peroxide and toothbrush she had used to clean the blood off the gauntlet remained. The supplies lay next to the towel she cleaned it on to catch the bloody runoff mixture. She walked to the island and lowered herself, taking her seat on the floor.

This was an inconvenience. She hadn't planned on going anywhere today. Eventually, she would have to leave the house again. She'd have to charge her phone. She needed to see if there was any news on the translation from Remus. She hadn't ate since before the party and wasn't sure if there was anything in the house to eat. That barely crossed her mind. The only thing that was going to get her out again was contacting Remus, but she hadn't wanted to do that until the pain in her wrist was manageable.

The visit from the detectives changed all that. If it was routine, why were there so many cops? If they were going to trust her to come down to the station on her own, why did six of them show up for the visit today? There was something they were hiding. They didn't have enough evidence yet to arrest her, but they knew. They had to.

Chapter Twenty-Four

Vanessa

Eileen closed the door after watching the police leave. They had told her to take her time to clean up, but there wasn't enough time or working facilities in her home to do that properly. She went back to the kitchen where her the contents of her open backpack spilled onto the floor. She picked up an outfit she had already worn and gave it the smell test. It wasn't too bad. As long as no one came real close, it should be fine. She slipped it on and wondered what to do next.

How much time was needed to get ready? Were they expecting her with styled hair and a full face of makeup? That wasn't happening any time soon. She needed a way to kill time, to make it appear as if she at least showered.

'Two nights, huh? There's plenty of stink to wash off me then, but I haven't the mind nor the energy to deal with it.'

She grabbed her cell phone and charger along with the change from the twenty she broke at the gas station then went out the front door, walking past the bloody clothes still laying on the floor. The front door clicked shut behind her, and she didn't stop to bother with the padlocks. The keys to them were somewhere in the house, but she couldn't remember where she put them. She couldn't even remember coming in through that door, not really, just a vague recollection which might not have been from the last time she came to the house. It could've been a previous time pushing its memory to the forefront of her mind.

The truck stop wasn't far, and it was a good a place as any to sit and wait. At least she could charge her phone there. None of the wait staff on this shift recognized her. Why would they? It wasn't her usual time during the early bird special hours. She still requested booth twelve. The waitress scrunched up her face, but took her to that booth nonetheless.

She told the waitress she'd just have water earning another disappointed look from her. When the woman walked away, she plugged the charger for her phone into the outlet on the wall under the table. No one had ever said anything to her before about using it, but she had a feeling this waitress might.

The menu lay spread on the table, and her eyes darted between the sides and the all-day breakfast. It was all she could afford. She tried to avoid looking at the pictures of the meals. It would be hard to resist temptation. Once she dipped into her stash, it would be too easy to keep spending it. Besides, the pictures always were a far cry better looking than what was served.

French fries sounded good. Once she had them, she craved them constantly. Between the dinner Remus bought her and the Burger Shack, she hadn't been able to get the taste of fries out of her cravings. It took forever for the waitress to bring them out after she ordered. For a short while something took her mind off the pain in her wrist.

She ate them slowly, wanting to savor them. The pain in her left arm began throbbing as soon as the first fry was popped into her mouth. The constant pain was bad enough, but the occasional throb sent waves of pain up her arm. Then it was unbearable. After she left the police station, she'd have to break down and be checked out at the hospital for another x-ray.

She'd lie and say she fell again and put her arm out to brace herself out of habit. The worst they could do was put a cast on it which worried her. If she couldn't manage to keep the splint, she'd cut the cast off at home. It sounded like a good plan, and she refused to allow herself any thoughts on what exactly she'd use to cut through it. The hospital she preferred would fill a prescription on site before you were discharged, or they used to anyway. She hoped they still had the pharmacy in house.

Halfway through her plate of fries, she turned her phone on to check for messages from Remus. She kept it plugged in because it wasn't charged near enough yet, but it prevented her from eating the fries too quickly. There were a couple voice mails from him, checking on her, wanting to see how she was holding up, and telling her not to give up hope. Have faith.

While she was checking her messages, a text notification came across her phone from Remus in all caps. *IT'S TRANSLATED!!* It was followed quickly by another text. *I will call you as soon as I talk to him. We're almost there. Just a little longer.*

It was all she could do to keep from calling him immediately. She had to threaten herself with taking the fries away if she dialed the number, as if it were something she'd actually follow through with, but it still worked. This put going to the emergency room on the back burner. Eileen grinned wildly and sat up straighter. She popped another fry in her mouth and considered not going to the police station at all. The problem was she didn't know yet what she'd been doing wrong. She didn't know what she'd have to do or how long it would take. Did the sacrifice have to coincide with a certain phase of the moon? Was there an incantation she had to recite?

A treatment that needed to be done to the body?

Just in case it wasn't something she'd be able to manage tonight she decided she'd still talk to the police unless Remus gave her news that would change her mind before then. She didn't want them tracking her down again because she never showed up unless she was already long gone.

The fries didn't last nearly as long as she'd have liked, and she thought about how great they tasted. Such a simple food. Easy to make. Far overlooked as an American delicacy in her opinion. The potato was probably the best discovery history had ever made when it came to food. Next to bacon of course.

Eileen had traveled overseas many times. The food there was very diverse. That's not to say it's bad by any means. Some of the foods over there were better. There were some meals she's had in Europe that were among the favorites of what she's ever had. It was just... different. The types of food they eat, the seasonings they use, the preparation, it was all unique by comparison.

Somehow, her mind connected the American food she was leaving behind to the last meals prisoners get on death row. Probably because the threat of being arrested had been real for a little while. What would her last meal be? Her thoughts fluttered between the lamb she had at the country club, pulled pork she had at a little dive joint in Chicago, or maybe the blackened fish she had just outside of New Orleans. They were all places she'd travel again just for the eats and wondered if inmates could get their last meal flown in to the prison. None of those she'd be able to get here. If she was guaranteed Noah would be resurrected tonight and had to pick a final American meal before flying out, french fries would be a good enough last meal to satisfy her.

She looked at her check. It was a little over three dollars after tax. It was a ridiculous price to pay for a cut up potato, but it was a steal for salty fried goodness on a plate. She put a five dollar bill on top of the ticket, grabbed her phone and tucked the charger in her bag then left.

She debated about going to the police station right away or waiting for Remus to call first. It could take hours yet, or he might not call until the next day. He hadn't given her an idea of when she'd here from him. Just that it'd be soon. The longer she had to wait the more excited and nervous she'd get, pacing the floors of her house all night. It'd be better to get the police department out of the way when she still had the nerves to act calm around an entire precinct of cops.

The detectives' names from the earlier visit had escaped her. *'Was it Carson?'* That didn't sound quite right. *'Maybe Johnson?'* The other detective she was fairly certain was named Woods. Was she only meeting with one of them or both?

Inside the station, she could see the top of a man's head sitting behind a counter. There was a glass window with a small circular speak way near the bottom. She walked up to it, and said, "Hi. My name's Eileen McBride."

"Have a seat," the man said before she could say anything more. "Detective Larson is expecting you."

'Larson,' she thought. She had been close.

There were two other people waiting, and she took an empty chair, sitting away from both of them. One of them looked perfectly at ease sitting around a police station which wasn't necessarily a compliment. The other was crying, and Eileen wondered who it was this woman was crying over and what they had done. Neither of the two were in cuffs. It wasn't like what's shown in movies where they cuff the suspect to a chair or pipe and leave them.

The door next to where the man behind the counter sat was across from Eileen, and she kept a close eye on it, waiting for it to open. She hoped it wouldn't take long for someone to collect her, and thought about asking if there was an idea of when it would be.

It was a different door across the room that finally opened. She almost had to strain her neck to watch who exited. The detective was one of the two who'd been to her house, but he was with Vanessa.

She didn't look too upset for someone who had just lost her husband. Spouses are always at the top of the suspect list, but the smile on the woman's face would keep her there if Eileen had been the one handling the investigation. *'Of course, she is inheriting a fortune. Money like that can brighten anyone's day, even a grieving widow.'*

After the accident, after she lost the baby, all the tabloids rumored the reason they didn't try again was because Vanessa was having second thoughts about having a child with him. His drinking and his gambling were out of control. He was losing to his addictions. They all painted her as a gold digger who stayed because of his money.

"If you need anything at all, don't hesitate to call," he told her. "Be happy to help."

Vanessa thanked him for everything and insisted the department had gone above and beyond already.

"Take care of yourself," he said. "You need to take it easy in your condition."

She touched her hand to her stomach, almost instinctively and possibly without realizing she'd done it. "Oh, yes, definitely."

Eileen dropped her eyes and turned her head away. The woman was pregnant. It was a mere observation. She didn't feel for her in any way. She wasn't happy for her that she was expecting. She wasn't saddened for her that she'd be a single mom. She also didn't feel any guilt for making her one. The fact Vanessa was pregnant made no more difference to her than the fact the sky was just starting to darken into an off teal shade of dusk. It just was. Life continued on after death every day.

"He had always wanted a son like we were going to have before..." Vanessa said. The sadness for her lost pregnancy could be felt in her voice even if the loss of her husband could not. She crossed fingers on both her hands. "Here's hoping."

"How far along are you?" the detective asked.

"I don't know," Vanessa said. "I still had to schedule an appointment with my doctor. I just took a home test yesterday."

Eileen couldn't bring herself to be excited for her. She couldn't be excited for anyone who gets to have a child in this unfair world where hers was taken from her. She hadn't been able to look at a mother since Noah's accident without feeling jealousy, anger, resentment, or a mix of all of it.

She wondered if the child was even his. The tabloids also hinted at allegations of infidelity. She glanced around nervously wondering if anyone could tell what she was thinking. It wasn't unreasonable to wonder about it. From what she saw at the house, they weren't sharing a bedroom. It wasn't proof by any means then. Many couples separate while they work things out, but they would still date, still get physical.

"Oh, so it's still early then?" The detective's voice brought her attention back to the police station.

"Maybe. We weren't trying again yet. The morning after..." Her voice choked up, and she stopped herself from finishing the sentence. "I could feel it. Something was different. So I bought a test and sure enough," she smiled weakly. She cradled her abdomen with both hands, and said, "It's like this baby was his last gift to me. A going away present."

The detective watched Vanessa as she left then noticed Eileen waiting. He smiled at her and held up one finger, signaling her to hold on. He walked to the floating head behind the counter and spoke to him quietly. The voices were too low for Eileen to make out, but the head did glance her way. She assumed the detective was letting the man know he was taking her back.

"Mrs. McBride." Detective Larson clasped his hands together as he walked her way.

"Eileen," she said. Changing her last name had never been on her list of priorities after the divorce, but it should've been. She didn't hear it much. It wasn't delivered to her mailbox every month anymore printed on a couple dozen bills. She almost forgot it was her name at all. She'd heard it said more that day than she had the previous two years combined.

"Thank you for coming out."

"I didn't realize it was optional," Eileen confessed. The snotty attitude had surprised her. It came out of nowhere. Perhaps it was because the pregnant widow could float out of here on cloud nine, going home to the millions that were now hers to control. Meanwhile, she still had to convince these fools her broken arm was no match against an NBA star, albeit a former one.

The detective laughed as though it was a joke. It irritated her even though she should be thankful he mistook her attitude for humor.

"If you come with me, I should be able to get you on your way back home before you know it," he said. "Do you need any help?"

Eileen wanted to smart off, to tell him it was her arm that was broken not her feet. She thought better of pushing her luck any farther. She shook her head and stood up. The detective brought her to the door Vanessa had just left through and opened it for her.

• • • •

'

Chapter Twenty-Five

Push

Eileen followed the detective through the door and down a maze of hallways. He led her to a room that looked more like a conference room than the interrogation room she expected, but then again, she wasn't under arrest. She took a seat near the door and placed her purse on the table next to her car keys. It was all she brought in with her. She had to pile some stuff into the purse to fill it out since she never used one anymore, dragging the book bag everywhere instead.

Her phone vibrated just then, and she took it out of her purse. It was Remus. *Figures he would have the information she needed now after she's already with the detective.* She rejected the call and placed the phone on the table next to her purse.

There was a television mounted to one wall showing the news. The reporters were talking about the missing girl who had been found. "...still no leads, and the young girl hadn't recovered her memory of everything that happened from her disappearance to when she was found. Was she covering for her abductor? Was this a case of Stockholm Syndrome? We'll hear from criminal psychologist, Dr. Morgan Banks later."

Detective Larson shut the door and adjusted the blinds on the windows to the hallway, closing them for privacy. It was just the two of them in this large room. She hoped no one else was joining them.

"But first," the anchor said, "Basketball star William Tucker, local legend and hometown hero..."

Eileen safely rolled her eyes while the detective had his back to her. *'Basketball star? Only because he's from here. No one else even remembers him.'*

"...found dead in his home two nights ago," he continued.

Two nights. The timeline still confused her. It was last night. That's when she crashed the party and snuck into his house.

On the screen was a picture of Tucker with his year of birth and death overlaid on it. He was younger than she'd have guessed. The picture was taken shortly after he was drafted. She hadn't realized, hadn't cared how much he had aged until she saw the younger version of him staring at her.

"The police are keeping tight lipped about this investigation..." Then she couldn't hear anymore. The reporter was still on the screen, and his mouth was moving. There was no sound.

Detective Larson set the remote back on the table after muting the news. "Sorry about that," he said.

Her phone rang again. It was Remus.

'He's probably heard of Tucker's death by now. That might be why he's calling.'

"Do you need to get that?" Larson asked.

"No, it's just a friend." She rejected the call again.

Remus sent a text, saying, "I really need to talk to you."

She placed the phone face down on the table. The detective didn't need to see anything else Remus might have to say.

Detective Larson sat down across from her. He was eyeing the splint on her arm again. She decided to baby it a little. It did hurt, so she didn't see anything wrong with emphasizing it. When she brought her right hand up to nurse it, he noticed her bracelet.

"That's interesting," he said, pointing at it.

Interesting was the polite way of saying something's ugly.

"Oh," Eileen smiled. "I found it at a flea market." The lies were coming to her on the spot. "Something about it fascinated me. I can't seem to take it off for long. It's like it begs me to keep wearing it."

Larson said, "Yeah, I can see that," like he wanted to say, "Do what you want with your ugly stuff."

What he finally said was, "I just have a few questions for you. Were you and the victim on good terms?"

"Huh," Eileen huffed loudly.

The detective shot her a glance. He realized the routine question he had asked hundreds of times had come out without thinking. "There was some bad blood between the two of you."

"Bad blood? More like my son's blood." Eileen stared at him. "Well, that is the reason I'm here isn't it?"

"What are your thoughts on that?" Larson asked.

"If I wanted to kill him, I'd have done it a long time ago."

Larson nodded and moved on. "When was the last time you saw Tucker?"

Without thinking about it, Eileen glanced at the television. It was a commercial. "In person?" She didn't wait for an answer. "It had to be the trial. I don't remember ever bumping into him anywhere else."

"And where were you two nights ago?"

'Two nights.'

"During his wife's birthday party," Larson continued. "Friday night into Saturday morning?"

'Where was I two nights ago? Or where was I the night of the

party?' Eileen was beginning to think it was a trick to see if she slipped up and said something incriminating.

"I usually keep to myself."

"So no one can vouch for your whereabouts?"

She hesitated before answering. Remus would cover for her, but she didn't want to drag him into it. There was still the broken arm on her side, making the police think she wasn't capable of overpowering Tucker, but it had worsened. "No, I was home. Alone."

The translation was almost complete. Even if they wanted to arrest her, she'd have her son and be out of the country before they could.

Larson closed the notebook he was writing in and thought for a moment. "Can I get you something to drink? Water, coffee, a soda?"

Soda. It had been a long time since she had it. She'd never drank it a lot, but it sounded good tonight. "Yeah, I'll take a cola," she said.

"What kind?"

"Anything but diet."

Larson left the room as her phone vibrated again. It was another text from Remus. "We had it all wrong."

'We?'

Remus was the one who had been wrong since the beginning. She looked at the television. Captions ran across the bottom of the screen, struggling to keep up with the images.

Larson returned and set the soda on the table in front of her. "Did you want a glass?"

"No," she said. "The can is fine."

He sat down again, and asked, "Where were we?"

Eileen opened the tab on the can and took a drink. The carbonation burned her mouth. The drink was sweet. It was one of a million little things she missed.

There was a loud bang down the hallway, and Eileen jumped, spilling some of the soda on her hands. It wasn't a gunshot. It sounded more like something being thrown or knocked over.

"Excuse me," Larson said. He left to investigate, not waiting for her reply.

When he opened the door, she could hear screaming. Multiple voices at once yelling at someone.

She looked around, but there was nothing in the room to help her clean up. Her baby wipes were in the book bag in her car. She set the can down and licked the soda off her fingers. Then she wiped her hands on her clothes.

Shouts could be heard not far away. They weren't right outside the door, and she couldn't hear exactly what was being said. Enough came through for her to make out someone was being detained.

Her phone had been vibrating off and on, so she checked it. "Where are you? I need to talk to you." It was Remus. It was always Remus. He was the only one she heard from anymore.

"I'm busy right now," she finally replied. She put the phone down on the table and sighed. There had to be something else to it. That's why Noah hadn't come back yet. There was some missing element, something else that costs money, something else they'd have to track down. It probably required a trip to the middle of the jungle only reachable by helicopter for some rare plant she'd have to anoint her son in for it to work. God only knows what that price tag would be. There was nothing left to sell besides the house itself. She practically already lived like a homeless person. Might as well make it official.

'Helicopter?'

"Oh, no." A tear rolled down her cheek. *Please let me be wrong.* A news article she had read not long ago came to mind, and she couldn't shake this bad feeling brewing in the pit of her stomach. She wanted to be wrong more than anything.

She watched the news, wondering if it'd be wrong to unmute it. They were covering the story of the girl again. She couldn't remember anything from the lost time, but she had been certain her abductor was going to murder her.

"With the discovery of Chuck Rogers's body," the reporter said, "it's believed somebody freed the young girl. Whether this person was involved and knew of the girl's existence this whole time, or this was someone who just discovered her and freed her, we don't know."

Both cheeks streaked with tears while she read the words at the bottom of the screen. "Evidence was found inside the home that belonged to the young girl. The police aren't releasing too many details right now..."

This had to be the first victim. There hadn't been enough to convict him, and the girl's body was never found.

Her phone vibrated, but she ignored it.

Eileen removed the bracelet from her wrist and pushed the eye. She watched the blade emerge. There was the man who claimed to be a pilot from the Vietnam War. She pushed the button again, and the blade disappeared.

Then the little girl came out of the woods with no memory of anything since the night she was kidnapped. *Push.* The blade appeared.

An image of Vanessa cradling her bumpless belly flashed in her mind. *Push.* The blade was gone.

The shouting had quieted down, but she could still here the voices of the officers. They were loud and dripping with adrenaline. Larson would be back soon.

Eileen saw the face of the homeless man, panicked and afraid while she stabbed him. *'The dagger doesn't bring back someone you know.'*

Push.

Chuck Rogers had put up a fight. It made her left wrist twinge just thinking about it. *'The dagger doesn't bring back someone you're thinking about when you die.'*

Push.

Vanessa had miscarried the night of the accident. That's why Tucker was in a hurry and not paying attention. He was trying to make it home to her. *'The dagger doesn't bring back the person whose life you took.'*

Push.

Her phone vibrated almost continuously. One message after another from Remus was being delivered. She didn't need to see them. She knew what he was going to say.

Eileen was bawling uncontrollably. This wasn't what was supposed to happen. *'The dagger brings back the person you miss the most, the person you want to come back to life.'*

Tucker longed for his son. *Push.* He was guilt ridden over not being there and blamed himself. That's why he didn't fight her.

Rogers was a nasty perverted old man who had probably hurt a number of children, but that missing girl was the first. She had watched enough true crime to have learned the first victim was almost always someone you cared for deeply.

Push.

She didn't know the homeless man's story. The man who walked out of the jungle could've been anyone from a lover to a really good friend. Maybe the homeless man believed his life would've been different if not for what happened and wished he wasn't dead every day.

Push.

The detective was talking to someone near the door. If she had listened to what was being discussed, she'd have heard them talking about getting a search warrant for her house. They had something on her, some detail she had overlooked. This new piece of information was just discovered as luck would have it with her already there of her own free will. It wouldn't matter.

She had to act quickly before he returned. She might not get another chance.

Remus was still trying to reach her. Her phone buzzed and buzzed. She wanted to throw it across the room. She had already figured out what he was trying to tell her. The dagger wasn't meant to be used for murder. It's for sacrifice.

Eileen set the bracelet in her lap and took off the splint. For a fleeting second, her wrist breathed a sigh of relief then the throbbing pain flooded her arm. It wouldn't hurt for much longer.

She put the bracelet in her left hand. It hurt to grasp it, and she used the table for support.

All she ever wanted to do was see Noah again, to hold him, to tell him how sorry she was for not being there for him that night. The blade dug into her right wrist, and she pulled it up her arm. The blade was sharp which made it easier to manage. Pain seared through her arm, and blood poured over her leg and onto the floor.

Her phone vibrated. She bit her lip to prevent her sobs from becoming too loud. Remus was telling her, "There has to be another way," but she didn't read it.

The detective was right outside the door now, and she prayed he didn't make it to her in time to stop her, to save her.

She took the bracelet in her blood covered right hand and dug the blade into her left wrist. Her right hand didn't cooperate. It wouldn't move like her mind was commanding it too. She had to drag her left arm against the blade and barely had enough strength to retract it when she was finished.

Eileen wouldn't be there to hold Noah, but she could ensure he had the chance to live again. The last thought she had before losing consciousness was that Noah should be pushing his way out of the mausoleum at any moment.

"Don't do anything rash," was the next text from Remus. Eileen never heard the phone vibrate.

She didn't see Detective Larson walk into the room muttering about how crazy it had been that night because of the full moon. He shut the door and looked at her. The realization of what she had done, of what had happened under his watch hit him slowly at first and then shot off like a firecracker, exploding in his mind.

Her chin was dropped to her chest. Her arms hung limp at her sides. Pools of blood collected on the floor underneath each hand. The bracelet she had been wearing lay on the table next to her splint.

Somewhere across town a little boy woke up screaming for

his mama.

Available everywhere in eBook, Paperback, and on Kindle Vella

The Elementals Series

Air

Earth

Fire

Water

Balance

Ravenwood

Volumes One - Three

The Below: Phillipe's Revenge

The Below: Mezzie's Prison

The Below: John's Duel

Fogpoint Harbor

The Inheritance

Buried Secrets

The Sacrificial Dagger

Line of Sight

Fairytale Horror
Blasse Haut: A Snow White Retelling

About the Author

Jennifer Lush is a mother of three from central Illinois where she has lived her entire life. Aside from spending time with her children and grandchildren, writing and traveling are her two main consuming passions. Luckily, they are mutually beneficial.

Writing has always been in her blood even if it took her longer than planned to do it. One of her earliest memories of longing to be an author happened in kindergarten when she told her parents what she wanted to be when she grew up. It took close to four decades, but she has finally made that childhood dream come true.

Jennifer is an entertainer at heart who is always making those around her laugh. She can turn any mundane event into a story worth repeating with flair. Inspiration for her fictional worlds comes from everywhere. There are more ideas floating through her mind than she has time to write, but she is determined to finish as many as possible.

Twitter: AuthorJLush
IG: AuthorJenniferLush
Tik Tok: AuthorJenniferLush